From Mourning into Gladness

From Mourning into Gladness

A Novel by

Carolyn Gilliam

www.FromMourningIntoGladness.com

ISBN 978-0-9833873-0-5

First Edition

Printed in the United States of America

Dedication

This book is dedicated to my mother, who encouraged me to try to do anything I chose, and my father, whose creative mind and adventurous spirit I inherited.

Acknowledgements

I was telling some of my fraternity sisters at an Alpha Phi Alumnae meeting about this book when a talented muralist and illustrator offered to do the cover. Thank you, Michelle Morse, for your superb work.

My special appreciation goes to Kimberley Westfall, who lent her formidable talents as an editor to make sure this book was "a good read."

Table of Contents

PART I

The Unthinkable

The sun had not yet peeked over the barren Judean hills outside Bethany when Deborah left her home, husband and son to begin her lonely trek. Women did not usually travel alone. Her husband had wanted to accompany her as he had always done, but this journey was different.

The fear of what she would find when she arrived in Bethlehem made her resolute in her decision to make this a solitary excursion. Her daughter's home was so small that there would be no room to accommodate more than one guest and she was certain that she would need to stay for some period of time.

Maybe a week. Maybe longer. There was no way to know.

She pulled her mantle closer against the chill of the early morning in this desolate area. She was no longer the slender girl who had happily followed the small herd of goats her family had when she was a child. She never had to watch her step then. Now, however, she was older and worse for the wear. Her body was stocky from bearing six children. The path was steep and very stony. Sometimes when she wasn't looking closely, her foot slipped off a rock. Not wanting to twist her ankle, she made her way slowly.

She had given her husband, Daniel, five strapping sons and a beautiful daughter. The first four sons were married with their own families. Although they lived in Bethany, they had taken up other trades, so they were living more separated lives. Her daughter, Rachel, had married a farmer from Bethlehem and the distance between them had kept them apart for long periods of time. Still there was an unusually strong bond between mother and daughter. Rachel always sent word when something important happened in her life, like the birth of her first son, Jacob, and more recently, the arrival of her second son, Reuben.

Deborah's youngest son, Samuel, was not as boisterous as his brothers. He was closest to Rachel, both in age and temperament. The two youngest offspring had also been closer to their parents, which was the reason Samuel was the one Daniel taught to follow the family trade and become a potter. The two of them worked well together. Samuel was as eager to learn the potter's trade as Rachel was to learn Deborah's homemaking skills.

Carefully picking her way along the little-used stone-strewn path, a shortcut to the road she would take, she thought back to the unbelievable events which had necessitated this sudden, solitary trip.

Yesterday had begun like any other market day. Daniel and Samuel had loaded the cart in the damp early morning for the trip to the Jerusalem marketplace where they would sell their wares. It was their custom to leave about dawn, arrive at the market midmorning and set up the displays of their pots, ewers, oil lamps and miscellaneous pottery items. They were expert potters with a reputation for the quality of their work and had developed a large following of customers. Normally, their cart would be empty by early afternoon and they would stop at an inn for some refreshment and talk with friends before returning to their home in Bethany in the early evening.

But that day, Deborah, busy at the loom, had been surprised when the pair arrived home in mid-afternoon. When she heard their hushed voices as they put up the donkey and cart, she began to worry. What had happened today to bring them home so early? Had there been a catastrophe which had destroyed their stock? She thought of all manner of things which could have happened, but she hadn't been prepared for the news they brought.

"Mother," Samuel exploded as he came through the door, "you'll never guess what Herod did yesterday!"

"You're right," she answered as she put down the shuttle and turned to listen, "nothing that monster does ever makes sense, so I could never guess. Is that what brought you home so early?"

He continued, "Yesterday Herod sent his troops to Bethlehem and they killed all the babies!"

"All the babies?" Deborah gasped, unable to believe her ears. "He killed all the babies? Why?"

"No," Daniel answered as he came through the doorway, "only the baby boys. We hurried home to tell you, because we knew you would be worried about Rachel and her young ones."

"All the baby boys," Deborah repeated, still trying to grasp the meaning of what they said. "All the baby boys?"

"Yes, Mother," Samuel continued. "Everyone was talking about it!"

"There were many versions, but as close as we could tell, this is what happened," Daniel interjected. "A few days ago, some magi from the East came to Herod and asked him where the new king of the Jews had been born. Of course, Herod, not being a Jew, didn't know anything about it, so he told his scribes to look it up and they came back and told him that the prophet Micah had prophesied that the birth of the Messiah would take place in Bethlehem.

"Well, Herod told the magi that it was to be in Bethlehem and asked them to return after they had found the child and tell him where it was so that he, too, could go worship him."

Samuel interrupted. "When they didn't come back after a couple of days, Herod figured out that they weren't coming and went into his usual frenzy."

Daniel continued, "He couldn't have a usurper to his throne around, so he had to kill him. The trouble was that he didn't know where the baby was, other than in Bethlehem. He didn't know when he had been born, either, so he just ordered every baby boy in Bethlehem under the age of two years to be killed and sent a detachment of his troops to do the deed."

"Oh my Rachel," Deborah wailed as the horror of the tale sunk into her mind. "Oh, my poor Rachel. Could she have escaped the terror? Could her babies be safe? Could God's providence have saved her family? I must go to her immediately."

"No," Daniel said firmly as he caught her arm, "not tonight. We'll pack the animal and set off early tomorrow morning."

Deborah nodded. Daniel was the head of the household and she knew that it was too late in the day to undertake the trip. She would use the night to make preparations and start at dawn, but she wanted to go alone. The men would only get in the way.

During the evening they discussed the trip. Normally, Deborah deferred to Daniel, but she wasn't afraid to make a point she thought was important. Nor was she shy about pressing her point if she was convinced that she was right. He was a good man and didn't want his wife to travel alone.

"It is not seemly for a woman to be traveling alone," Daniel said.

"There will probably be many other women going on the same solitary journey, so that I will not be really alone. And I will make the entire trip in daylight on a busy road," Deborah answered and before he could respond, reminded him, "There will not be enough room in Rachel's small house either and I may have to stay for a few days."

Daniel shrugged his shoulders and stepped outside the door. Deborah was an assertive woman who had made her point and he realized that it was futile to discuss it any further.

Most of the night, Deborah worked preparing the food she had on hand for the men to eat while she was gone. She ground the wheat that was in her storage jar and made bread from it. She cooked lentils and beans and added some lamb to make a stew. With the eggs which the chickens would lay, the food she had prepared would feed them for a few days and perhaps she would be back by that time. If she wasn't, their other sons' wives would see that they were fed.

Deborah gathered the few belongings she would take to sustain her visit and finally lay down by Daniel for a few hours of sleep. Before dawn, she arose, packed some dates and bread to take with her, made her final preparations, said goodbyes to her reluctant husband and son and was on her way a little before the sun rose. She would reach her destination by early afternoon.

When I reach the main road from Jerusalem to Bethlehem, she thought, the walking will be easier. It will be packed down by the traffic that uses this main road to Hebron, passing through Bethlehem. As she topped the hill above the road, Deborah saw what she had expected, a number of women traveling alone in the same direction she would head.

Ordinarily, when women traveled, they were accompanied by men and families, but she knew that these solitary women were on the same mission. She joined the grim-faced procession. There was no communication, even with their eyes. Each one trudged on with their eyes on the road and their thoughts in Bethlehem.

At mid-morning, one by one, the women each found a place to sit in silence for a while and eat their morning meal. One woman just sat there and cried. No one came to comfort her. She was left in her own little world, even as the others stayed in their solitary worlds. Shortly, their bodies refreshed a bit, they continued the long and dreadful walk.

As she started down the last hill in her journey, Deborah looked across the broad valley. In the distance she could see Herodium, the man-made fortress built by Herod to be his summer palace. It had been built by the uneasy monarch to give him a refuge near Jerusalem to which he could flee if his subjects turned on him. This fear was one which could be very real because Herod was an Idumean, whose ancestors were descendents of the Edomites. For centuries the Jews had held an intense animosity for them and now the Roman conquerors had made him the king over them. Herod was a jealous ruler, but a cunning master builder whose ambitions drove him to many enormous projects. He had not only built the large Roman-style port city, Caesarea, but had even built a long aqueduct to bring water many miles from the hills and enclosed an artificial safe harbor for the trading ships from many nations making it an important sea port. He also built palaces at Masada, Machaerus, and Jericho.

He was as sly as his father, too, including in his projects the building of a great Temple for the Jews which he intended to rival the Temple built by Solomon. This project, which had begun twelve years ago by enlarging the level surface with the placement of huge stones around Mount Moriah, was intended to keep the Jews satisfied with his reign and compliant with his rule. As long as he was making progress on this building, he knew that his subjects would not rebel. It might take a very long time to complete.

On the plain surrounding the breast-shaped man-made mountain that was Herodium were the mansions built by the elite who pandered to the king. To be an official in Herod's court assured one of great wealth, for Herod bought allegiance. The sight of all that affluence caused anger to well up in Deborah. Herod had everything and all the poor villagers had were their children. Now that monster had taken these most precious treasures away from them. His fear of losing his crown had driven him to murder members of his own family, so it followed that he would brazenly order the killing of others without a second thought.

Looking ahead at her destination, Deborah was once again reminded why Rachel had been so happy in Bethlehem. The village sat perched atop one of the low hills that are so much a part of Judea, surrounded by fields of wheat and pastures of sheep. The very name, Bethlehem, meant "House of Bread". It was the home of the famous shepherd-turned-king, David. The sheep raised in the area around Bethlehem were a main source for the sacrificial lambs sold at the Temple. These lambs had to be unblemished. The terrain surrounding the village was gentle and the shepherds were among the best in the nation. Bethlehem had provided a comfortable life for its inhabitants – until a few days ago.

As the women began the ascent into the town, its peaceful appearance from the distance changed. The stillness of the air was now filled with a loud wailing. The sound of mourning reached the ears of the women and changed their expressions. Tears began running down their cheeks. Jaws were more firmly set. Shoulders stooped as the feared possibility became real. Filled with dread, they trudged on, entering the village.

Along the streets were dried pools of blood and blood spatters were visible on every wall. The people who were walking in the village were distant, like walking dead men. The heart had gone out of this once vital town. Nearly every home was filled with mourning. Every family had been touched.

Deborah reached the far end of the town and turned down the street leading to the home occupied by her daughter, Rachel, her husband, Eli, and the two babies, Jacob who was nearly three, and Reuben, her suckling. Then she saw two patches of blood-stained earth near the door to their home and knew that Rachel and Eli had not escaped the bloodbath. Now there would be only Rachel and Eli. She knelt beside the stained earth and gently touched the soil, saying a prayer for each of the children. Tears welled up in her eyes. As she looked up, she saw Eli standing at the door.

"Come in, Mother," he invited.

Deborah couldn't speak past the lump in her throat, so she nodded her head, stood, wiping away her tears and entered as he stepped aside. With helpless hands Eli pointed to the corner and Deborah saw her daughter sitting, her legs drawn up to her chest and a vacant stare in her eyes. Her light brown hair was streaked with blood as her head covering had been lost in the street and blown away by the wind in that awful moment. Her clothes, too, were covered with the blood of her children.

Crossing the room, Deborah knelt beside her child, embraced her and began rocking back and forth, singing a childhood lullaby in a voice that cracked with grief. It was all she could think to do.

Eli watched his mother-in-law rocking his wife for a while and then went out the door. His eye was drawn to the blood-soaked earth in the street. Walking to it, he paused for a moment, then angrily thrust his foot on the place and rubbed it out of existence. Then he squatted near the door and aimlessly drew meaningless figures in the dirt. His mind was unable to make the pieces of his life fit together again. Everything had been so beautiful, so perfect, before those terrified screams changed it all.

Eli's Story

The turning point of Eli's life had been that joyous day he had accompanied his younger brother, Nathan and his wife, Rebecca, as they took their new son to the Temple for presentation to the priest on the eighth day after his birth. As the little group passed through the streets of Jerusalem to the Temple, a young woman dashed around a corner and ran into him.

"Are you all right?" he asked as he helped her to her feet.

"Yes, thank you," she replied.

"What is you name and where are you going?" he asked, mesmerized by her tender eyes and the golden brown hair shimmering in the sunlight.

"My name is Rachel," she had answered, "and I am running an errand for my father."

"Are you sure that you aren't hurt?" he pressed, not wanting to let her leave his presence.

"Come along, Eli," called Nathan as he and Rebecca began walking on.

"Where can I come to check on you later?" he asked her urgently.

Rachel answered, "My father and brother have the potter's booth in the marketplace."

When the ritual was over, Eli had excused himself, telling his brother and sister-in-law that he had an errand to run and would meet them later for the walk home. With a knowing wink, Nathan and Rebecca had gone on their way while Eli sought the potter's booth. There he saw Rachel. She was even more beautiful than before. She blushed when she saw him and walked toward him.

"What is your name – I forgot to ask," she said with a smile. She really hadn't thought that she would ever again see the handsomely ruddy man.

"Eli," he answered as he followed her toward her father.

"Father," Rachel said as her father turned to her, "I would like to introduce you to the man I nearly ran over this morning. His name is Eli."

Daniel gave a slight bow as he looked at the muscular young man walking up behind his daughter. He was a large, strong man with shoulders made broad and muscular. His face was sun-tanned and leathery, as were his arms and hands, but his eyes were gentle. "I have not seen you before in Jerusalem."

"No, I don't get to the city often. I am a farmer at Bethlehem."

"Do you own your fields?"

"No, I am the third son, but I really love to farm, so rather than take up another trade, I chose to work for a neighbor who has fine fields, but no son. I have worked for him for nearly ten years now."

"Will you be content to always work for another man?" Daniel asked.

"No," Eli answered, "in fact I am buying the fields from him now."

Daniel's eyes brightened. Good fields did not often become available for purchase as they were passed down from generation to generation within the family. The eldest son inherited the major share of the family's land and usually stayed on it to make his living. Younger sons received such small shares, that they usually sold their share to the older brother and took up other trades. "How is that?" he asked.

"About eight years ago, the man who owns the fields saw his last daughter marry and move away. Then his wife died and he has been very lonely. One day he asked me if I wanted to buy his fields from him. I had been praying for such an opportunity. He said that since I was such a fine worker, he would be willing to sell me the fields for ten years work, so in two more years I will own them and will be working for myself and my wife."

"Oh, then you are married," Daniel said.

"Not yet, but I plan to be when I find the right woman."

Rachel had been standing a few feet away while the men talked. She blushed when they turned to her and Eli's heart leaped.

"Where do you live?" Eli asked Daniel.

"We abide in Bethany. You will be welcome any time you can come," he replied.

"Rachel, I must be returning to my brother for the walk home now, but I'm glad we met and I hope to see you again soon," Eli said and he left.

After his fields were planted, Eli found many excuses to travel to Bethany and one day, he brought Rachel back with him to his mother's home as his betrothed. In due time, the wedding celebration completed the necessary ritual and they moved into their own home, the cozy one-room house Eli had built at the edge of Bethlehem near his fields. She had loved that she could see the fields from the doorway. It wasn't large in size, but it had everything a new bride could want and Rachel had seemed so happy to have her own home. She sang all the time. He loved to hear her song as he neared the house after a day in the fields. Theirs was truly a home filled with love.

For more than three years life had seemed to be heaven on earth. Rachel brightened his life every time he looked on her. Her cheerful disposition stayed with him as he toiled in the fields and seemed to make the hard work more worthwhile. She made the work even seem light when she worked alongside him. Then she and God had given him a fine son, Jacob, and then another, Reuben. Although she no longer worked with him in the fields, his heart was filled to overflowing with his little family.

As he did most every day, Eli had been working in the fields from dawn that fateful day, but because he was working in the far side of his fields, which were on the side of town away from Jerusalem, he had not seen the detachment of troops marching into the village. He had been completely unaware of what was taking place until he heard the first terrible wails. They were followed by more and the clashing sound of armor and horses. Eli dropped his tools and ran from the field, toward the town.

As he came to the edge of town he saw a mounted soldier, sword drawn, chasing a woman who was carrying a toddler in her arms. She darted into her home and closed the door, but the soldier, dismounted and threw it open. A great wail arose from the house and he came out a moment later, his sword bloodied. He remounted, wheeled his horse and charged back down the street, nearly knocking the stunned Eli from his feet.

"What is happening?" gasped Eli as he continued toward his home. "I must find Rachel and the boys and protect them." But as he turned the corner of his street, he saw a foot soldier approaching Rachel, who held Reuben in her arm and had Jacob in tow, heading for the door of their home.

Eli started running, but the soldier swung his sword and Jacob dangled limply from his mother's grasp. Then the soldier grabbed Rachel's shoulder and spun her around, knocking off her head covering and flipping the baby from her arm. The child had hardly touched the dirt street when he plunged his sword into him, spun on his heel and ran into Eli. Pushing him aside, the soldier continued down the street.

Staring in stunned disbelief, Eli watched as Rachel knelt beside the bodies of her sons, and pulled them to her. He shook himself out of his disbelief and hurried to her side, gently lifting Jacob and holding him to his chest. Tears streamed down his face as he held the lifeless body. Then he helped Rachel to her feet. She was still carrying Reuben as he led her into the house.

He took a linen cloth, laid it on the floor and placed Jacob on it. Then he laid a second cloth next to it and taking Reuben from Rachel's arms, laid him on it. Rachel just stood there, looking down silently. Eli spread their sleeping mat and led her to it. She made no cry, no sound. She just lay there so still, staring at the roof.

Rachel's Story

Rachel hummed a merry tune as she kneaded the dough for the bread. Life was good here in Bethlehem. She had moved here when she married Eli. He was a good provider, although it meant that he spent long hours each day working his fields. The weather had not been kind to them the past few years, so Eli's crops had only sustained them, not large enough to provide extra money with which to hire help. Still there was always hope that this year would be better. Indeed, this year the fields looked very good. There had been enough rain to give the plants a good start and the robust crop had every appearance of being very large, a good harvest, God willing.

Rachel had made the adjustments necessary when she had gone to Eli's home in Bethlehem as his betrothed. She had quickly come to love his mother and father. They were much like her parents. She had been glad that her mother had been so thorough in teaching her how to do the household duties. The relationship between Rachel and her mother-in-law had developed into a beautiful friendship and she had been devastated when Eli's mother became sick a few days after the wedding celebration and died. After her burial, his father had gone to live with his youngest son, who lived in Hebron.

Eli and Rachel loved their little house on the edge of the village, near his fields, a house of peace and contentment, away from the activity of the main road. There was only one other house on the short street and Rachel had enjoyed the company of the old widow who lived there, but had missed it since she died a year ago. She was glad that she had Jacob for company during the days. She never felt lonely with his presence.

Jacob was sitting in the corner, quietly playing. Rachel smiled, as she often did when she considered her son. As she placed the thin patties of bread dough on the hot baking jar to bake, she watched the toddler. Sometimes he drew things with his fingers on the floor, as he had seen his father do when he was contemplating something. But today, he was just sitting there looking expectantly. Nothing happened and in a few minutes, Rachel saw him lay his curly black-haired head down and fall asleep.

Rachel went about preparing the fruit and nuts, the slices from the mutton and the bowl of vinegar which would season the freshly baked bread. She set all these on the small table just outside the door under the extended roof. At just the right time, Eli appeared around the corner of the house and sat on the mat beside the table. After blessing the food, he ate. Rachel brought a cup of water from the jar and handed it to him.

"Refresh yourself," she said, "are you finished with the planting yet?"

"Not quite," he answered, "but I should be by tonight."

"This year looks to be good, doesn't it? The plants near the house are already up. I love the color of the new wheat."

"Yes, it looks like it is getting a good start. We've been blessed with rain at the right time this year. Praise be to God!"

When he had eaten, Eli returned to the fields. He would be home about sundown for the evening meal and until then Rachel would busy herself with household duties.

Before she tidied up the table, Rachel sat on the mat and ate her meal. It was pleasant to sit here and watch the wheat in the field at the end of the street. She loved the way the plants swayed back and forth in accompaniment to the wind. It was so fresh-looking in the light green of new wheat. Summer would darken the color and fall would change it to golden. Then the heavy heads would turn white and beckon the harvest. She said a silent prayer to God that this would be a good year, not only for the harvest, but also for her family in other ways.

Rachel was grateful that her home was near the village well. The water from Bethlehem's well was well-known as the best tasting water in all Israel. She took a long, slow drink of the clear liquid, allowing it to trickle down her throat. How refreshing it was! She knew how much King David had enjoyed doing this same thing, for he had written about it in a psalm. "As the deer pants for the water brook, so my soul longs for you, oh my God."

She thought again about her exciting news – her "harvest". What would the new baby be? Another boy to play and wrestle with his older brother and his father? To grow up strong and labor in the fields with Jacob and Eli? She knew how much Eli was looking forward to the day when Jacob would be alongside him in the fields. Her fair male child would someday be tanned like his father. What a handsome pair they would be! Now perhaps, there would be two sons alongside their father. What a blessing!

But maybe the new one would be a girl who would work beside her and be her companion and friend during the days. A friend she could teach to prepare meals and make clothes and do all the myriad of things it took to run a household, just as her mother had taught her. She knew that God would know best and she would gladly accept whatever He ordained.

Jacob awoke and came to her side. She knew that he, too, needed to eat, so she took him up onto her lap and fed him small pieces of the mutton and fruit. Soon he was satisfied and snuggled against her. He was nearly weaned, but occasionally she allowed him to suckle a bit. There wasn't any milk now, but the action was a comfort to both of them. In a couple of minutes, he wiggled off her lap and went to find some new activity in which to engage, so Rachel cleared the table and began her afternoon weaving.

She was making a new tunic for Eli. As she passed the shuttle back and forth, her thoughts drifted to the news she would tell Eli this night. She was now sure that there would soon be another baby. Eli would rejoice with her. They both considered children as God's special gifts. There would be even more laughter in the house and Jacob would have someone to play with as children play together.

The shuttle fairly hummed as the fabric took shape and soon the sun's rays through the lone window told Rachel that it was time to put away her weaving and begin preparations for the evening meal. Eli would soon be returning from the field and he would be hungry. She began the fire in her cooking jar. Eli loved her freshly baked bread, so she made it twice a day instead of the once most wives did. It was a little thing which pleased her husband and that fulfilled her.

As she mixed the flour she had ground that morning with salt, leavening and water, she found herself humming again. She couldn't hide the joy she felt as she contemplated the response from Eli on her wonderful news.

The Edict

There was great excitement in Bethlehem! A Roman soldier had delivered an edict from the Emperor in Rome requiring that all the people in Israel must return to the home of their ancestors and be registered. Although this action was taken to assure Rome that all taxes were being collected and Rome was getting its due, this was especially important for the village of Bethlehem. It was the birthplace of the great King David, who had many descendents, and all of them would be coming to Bethlehem!

Eli had quickly realized that this was orchestrated by God, because this year he would have a larger than normal harvest. His wheat would be needed to make bread for the great influx of people expected. He was glad that his ancestors had always lived in Bethlehem and so they didn't have to travel anywhere. He would be able to stay and work to ensure the proper selling of his crop.

It wasn't long before the baker approached him to contract for the crop. That meant that they would have enough money to tide them over the winter and still enough to be able to hire help for the next year. This prospect made him very happy, especially because of Rachel's news of the new baby expected in a few months. Now he could look forward to being with his family earlier in the evenings, instead of having to work from dawn to dusk as he had for so many years. God was good to them and he sang a song of praise to the Lord, thanking Him for this bountiful crop and asking for His continued blessings on his family.

At first, the registrars were efficient and travelers had to stay only a day or two, but as the weeks passed and more and more people descended on the village, the lines grew long and most of the visitors had to spend a week or more to get registered. The inns were turning away people and nearly everyone in town had guests staying with them. Sometimes they were relatives, but sometimes the travelers were renting space in private homes which enterprising owners had offered for a price.

Rachel wondered why the owner of the house across the street from theirs hadn't repaired the roof so that he could rent it to travelers, but it still remained as desolate as it had been since the day the old woman who had lived there died. That had been a year ago. She missed seeing the old woman, who had been her only neighbor on the short street. Her son, Jonah, had never even come to look at the place since her death.

Rachel and Eli had only one room and there was no usable roof on it, so they could not take advantage of this possibility for extra income. Rachel thought about what other ways they could use the sudden influx of visitors to better their circumstances.

Then she had an inspiration – she could make bread to sell to the people waiting in line to register. Eli would be glad to provide her with the wheat and she could arise earlier in the morning so that she could grind the wheat and bake the bread in the cooler morning hours. That way it would be very fresh and tasty when she approached the people standing in line to be registered. Buying the bread from her would allow them to avoid losing their places in line by having to go to the baker's.

When Eli returned home that night, Rachel excitedly laid out her plan to him and he marveled again that his wife was such an industrious, beautiful helpmate. Now she was willing to take on extra work at a time when she was also going to give him another child. What more could a man ask? He looked into her dancing eyes and drew her to him.

"If you're sure that this extra won't be too much for you, I think it is a wonderful plan," he assured her.

"The mornings are getting cool now and the heat from the cooking jar will take the early morning chill off the house," she told him with a wink.

Little Jacob didn't seem to notice that she was doing different things now. She was still close by and could keep an eye on him. He was such a good boy and amused himself. He knew every inch of their house, even where the mouse lived. Daily he carefully picked up some of the wheat that escaped the millstone when his mother ground it into flour for the bread. He thoughtfully laid it on the stone just outside the hole where the mouse lived, so that it would not have to venture into the house to find something to eat. Rachel found herself smiling again. How blessed she was to have Jacob!

It wasn't long before Rachel's fine bread had gained a reputation, passed from traveler to traveler and soon she was baking an amount that would have lasted her family nearly a month every morning. She began grinding the wheat before the sun arose and by the time she had ground enough for the day's requirements, it was time to prepare a morning meal for Jacob.

She now had two baking jars, so as soon as Jacob was fed, she kneaded the dough and patted out the patties, carefully placing them so that she could get the maximum number on each jar. By the time the first batch was baked, she had kneaded and patted out more dough. She carefully laid the finished bread in a basket and replaced it with the next batch. She repeated this routine six times each morning and barely finished in time to prepare the mid-morning meal for Eli, which she placed on the small table for him to eat when he came from the field.

When Eli came in, she took the basket and went to the registration line. She quickly sold all she had. Then she rushed back home to allow Eli to return to the fields. She wished that she had someone to watch Jacob while she sold the bread, but Eli didn't seem to mind having some time when he wasn't so tired to play with his son. Still, she knew that he would have to work harder to make up for the extra time he spent at home.

There was a niche in the corner above the place they spread their sleeping mat at night and that was where Rachel secreted the coins she earned from selling the bread. Each day, the niche was filled a little more and she began to dream about how she would spend the money. Perhaps she would have Jonas, the mason, build her a fine outdoor oven so that she could bake large loaves and sell them all the time. Or maybe she would buy a new prayer shawl for Eli. Or maybe some soft wool for a blanket for the new baby. It was fun to dream such lovely dreams while she worked to make them come true, but she knew that the coins she gathered and those Eli's crop brought would probably be used to add onto their house so that it would be sufficient for a growing family. That would be fine with her. God is so good, she thought.

The Miracle Night

Rachel was glad when these days drew to a close and she had her family gathered about her. The busyness of the days left her exhausted at night, but the comfort of the presences of her husband and son soothed away the fret of the day and she was ready to go to sleep as soon as they settled down. She lay next to Eli and drifted off to sleep thinking about her gratitude to God for all He had provided for them.

It was the middle of the night when Eli got up and went to the doorway. Rachel roused slightly from her slumber and heard the sound of many feet and the soft bleating of sheep. It sounded like they were passing down the main street of the town.

"What is it, Eli?" she asked.

"It looks like the shepherds are bringing their flocks to town early for market day, but they aren't stopping at the sheep market. They are going right down the main road," he said, returning to her side. "I'll go see what is going on."

As he stepped out into the street, Eli noticed how bright the night was. He always thought the full moon was bright, but this night seemed even more illuminated and it wasn't the time of the full moon. He looked up in the sky and saw many stars, but the radiant light wasn't coming from them. The sky seemed as brilliant as daytime. He returned to get Rachel.

"You must come and see the brightness of the sky," he told her, "I've never seen anything like it!" Rachel wrapped the blanket about her and followed him out the door. As they looked around, she saw that it was nearly as brilliant as at noonday. And he was right – she had never seen anything like it, either.

Hearing the bleating of the sheep at the end of the block, Eli took hold of her hand and started toward the sound, but Rachel pulled it out of his grasp.

"I'll get Jacob and meet you there. Maybe by the time I get there you will be able to find out what is happening," she said as she turned toward the house. Quickly gathering the sleeping child in her arms under the blanket, she rejoined Eli.

He was talking to one of the shepherds.

"It is too wonderful!" Eli exclaimed. "Rachel, one man said that these shepherds were tending their sheep tonight. They were remarking about the brightness of the night when a band of the angels of God appeared to them and told them that the Messiah was born tonight here in Bethlehem! Can you believe it?"

"The Messiah – here in Bethlehem!" she repeated.

"Yes," Eli replied. "I know that there is scripture saying that Bethlehem would be the birthplace of the Messiah, but, can you believe it? Could it really have happened tonight?"

Taking her arm, Eli led her into the mass of moving people and animals. They were not the only townspeople now in the procession. Every block more and more joined in. Yet there was a stillness, a reverence for this incredible event.

When the procession got to the inn, Rachel gasped.

"Surely the Messiah was not born in that awful noisy inn."

The crowd turned and went down a slope to the wide meadow which opened out from a cave where the innkeeper allowed his guests to stable their animals while they were lodging with him.

Eli told her what the shepherd with whom he had spoken said, "The angel told them that as a sign, we would find the Messiah lying in a manger."

"In a manger?" Rachel whispered to Eli. "Surely there is some mistake. God wouldn't allow His Son to be born in a dirty place where animals are kept, would He?"

"Apparently," Eli answered, "He would."

The shepherds stopped in front of the small cave below the inn. Just inside the doorway, Rachel saw a man and a woman with a new baby. The infant was tightly wrapped in cloths and lay quietly in a feed trough near the doorway. Straw had been placed in the trough and the young mother was looking with awe at her new son.

Rachel mused that she had never seen townspeople standing so close to the aromatic shepherds. Yet, tonight seemed to be a night of miracles, so she guessed that this was one, too.

The father came out and spoke briefly with one of the shepherds, then returned to the cave and spoke with the mother. One by one, the shepherds approached to within a few feet of the doorway and knelt. Bowing their heads, they prayed, then rose and left the scene. Each man's sheep followed him and after a while they had all gone. Some of the townspeople were still there and they, too, came forward and worshiped the child.

When Eli began to walk toward the cave, Rachel realized that they were the only ones left. She followed her husband and stood behind him, holding the still sleeping Jacob on her shoulder and bowed her head. Eli finished his prayer and they, too, left.

The brilliantly lit sky was so bright, that it lit the little house like daylight, making it hard for Rachel to go back to sleep. She was thankful that Jacob had slept through the whole event. Eli had knelt upon their return and thanked God for sending His Son and for allowing his family to be witnesses to this miracle, then he laid down next to Rachel and was soon sound asleep.

Rachel found herself wondering about the young woman who was the mother of this remarkable baby. Did she know that she would bear God's Son? She looked so very young. They were obviously travelers who probably came for the census. How and why had she made such a journey so close to her time of deliverance? She had so many questions, but finally drifted off to sleep still pondering them.

Mary's Story

Mary had been surprised when the shepherds, sheep and townspeople began to gather outside the entrance to the stable cave. She smiled at the tiny baby in the straw-filled feed trough beside her. This was surely not the place she had expected to give birth to the Messiah – the Savior of her nation. It was, however, another affirmation of the angel's message to her on that night that now seemed so long ago. The shepherds had told Joseph about the angelic visitation that had announced her son's birth and told them they would find him in a manger. So they had come to witness the miraculous event.

It was starting to seem real now, Mary thought. She remembered how she had been such a carefree, fun-loving girl only a year ago. She had loved to tease her brothers and her mother. They were just innocent annoyances. She smiled as she remembered.

"Mary," he had called that day. He always began with Mary, because she was always up to something. Still, Ezra loved his sister and thought of her as a bundle of mischief with twinkling eyes and a head full of curly black locks.

"Where's my sash?" he called again, "I'm meeting Michal and I'm in a hurry." Michal was her brother's betrothed.

"Why do you always call on me when something's amiss?" she had asked.

"Because you are usually the one who made it amiss," he answered. "Now where is it? Come on, Mary." He always found it hard to be angry with her. She was so like the frisky lamb he had taken for his own as a boy. She was full of life with not a serious bone in her whole body.

After she had produced the sash and Ezra left, Anne, her mother, put her arm around her shoulders and gave her a quick hug.

"Why do you torment your brothers?" she asked.

"Because I love them and want them to notice me. They are always so very busy and I want them to talk to me sometimes," Mary had answered. "Do you get angry when I tease you, Mother?'

"Sometimes, when it is ill-timed, but I know that you mean no harm by it, so I just try to love you all the more," she had answered.

She wasn't playful with her father. He was more likely to punish her for misdeeds, but mostly, she didn't tease him because she loved him so dearly and didn't want to cause him any trouble.

When Mary had told her mother about the visit from the angel, she had thought that it was one of Mary's stories and wouldn't believe her no matter how Mary tried to assure her that every word was true. Finally, she decided that she would drop the subject and treasure the wonderful knowledge of the visit in her heart until it came to pass – and she had no doubt that it would come to pass.

Mary would always remember that special night. She had been awakened by a restless spirit and had gone out to the nearby olive grove so the cool night air could clear her mind. She loved Abram's olive trees. They gave her a shady place to sit on a hot day and look across the Galilean countryside. There she daydreamed about her future. If she needed to be by herself to figure something out, she would come here.

As she sat under a gnarled olive tree, looking at the stars though its branches, she wondered what was bothering her. She heard the rustling of a little night animal, but couldn't see it. Not far away, she saw the village of Nazareth, its streets now empty and lonely. Suddenly the night seemed to glow and a man in white garments appeared before her.

"Do not be afraid," he said. "Mary, you are favored among women. The Lord God has selected you to be the mother of His Son, who will be born to you in due time."

Mary gasped. She could not say anything for a while, then she stammered, "But how can this be? I have never known a man."

The angel told her, "You will be overshadowed by the Holy Spirit."

"But," Mary asked, "what about Joseph, the man to whom I am betrothed? Will he not find me unfaithful to him?"

"Do not worry about Joseph," the angel answered. "He will know the truth at the right time."

The angel was gone as suddenly as he had appeared. Mary sat there alone under the tree. This wasn't a dream, she told herself. It was real, but still she found it hard to believe what she had been told. Was she truly the one chosen by God to bear the Messiah, the long-awaited Savior of Israel? For centuries, every girl in Israel had dreamed of being so honored. Was she really the one who would receive the blessing?

She was softly crying tears of astonishment at the amazing proclamation when she returned to her bed. The wonder of this revelation overwhelmed her and she was unable to sleep. The next morning, when she tried to tell her mother, it seemed so improbable, even to her. Maybe she had dreamed it after all. She knew that she couldn't tell Joseph. How could he understand? How could he believe her? She was still having trouble believing it had happened. The angel had left her with the feeling that she wouldn't have to tell him. Maybe the angel would speak to Joseph, too. Time would bear out whether it was a dream or not. In the meantime, she would continue to live as if the visit had never happened.

Mary had been betrothed to Joseph, the village carpenter, a few months earlier. As was the custom, she was now spending a great deal of time at Joseph's house, learning from his mother, Sarah, all the things she would need to know to please and care for her new husband. By the time the betrothal period ended, in about a year, she would be ready to make a home for Joseph. She was quick to learn the tasks Sarah showed her. She wanted to be a good wife. Her betrothed was a good man and, as a skilled carpenter who made an adequate living, had been considered the most eligible bachelor in the village of Nazareth. She was greatly honored that he had chosen her as his bride. Because he was older by a number of years, she had at first been a bit intimidated by him, but when they spent some time together at village functions, she saw how kind and sincere he was and a desire to please him replaced the reservations she had felt.

About four months after the angel's visit, Mary's mother received a letter from her cousin's husband, Zacharias, who was a priest in Jerusalem. Excitement filled the household as Esau, Anne's husband read aloud its contents.

"Peace and health to all in the household of Cousin Anne and her family.

"I, Zecharias, and my wife, Elizabeth, send glad tidings to you. Although we are both advanced in age, God is blessing us with a child. Your cousin is now in her sixth month and doing well. However, I feel that it would be best for her and the baby if she had a companion during this time. It is my preference that one of her relatives would do us the honor of filling this position. Would your daughter be willing to come to us for a period, to help in this capacity?

"We will await your answer. May it come quickly."

Anne spoke with her husband and together they went to talk with Sarah and Joseph about the request. They all agreed that this experience would be good training for Mary, who had been the youngest in the family and, therefore, had no real experience in the birth or caring for babies and Joseph looked forward to having a large family.

Mary had mixed feelings when they told her that she was to go to Kir Jarim, a village about eight miles northwest of Jerusalem. She would miss her days with Sarah and Joseph and her family, but she was excited about the trip and the new experience and responsibilities she would have there.

Joseph walked with Mary to Kir Jarim. At first Mary had literally danced around Joseph's steady stride. Her joy at this new chapter of her life lifted his spirits, but after the first day, she settled into his pace. It had taken them nearly a week to cover the distance between Nazareth and Kir Jarim. As they entered the town, they stopped at a vegetable vendor's stall and asked directions to the house of Zacharias, the priest. It was on the same side of the town and soon they were there.

When Joseph rapped on the door, a young servant girl answered and learning their names, ran off to call her mistress.

"Please come into the courtyard," Elizabeth bade as she approached the still open door. She led them to two benches under a tree and as they sat down, the servant girl brought them cool drinks.

"Did you have a good journey?" Elizabeth asked, but before the question was answered, Zacharias arrived.

"Zacharias cannot speak," Elizabeth explained. "The day we received the good news of this baby, he was serving in the Temple and received a visit from an angel announcing our son. When he showed disbelief, the angel struck him dumb, so he now talks by writing on a tablet."

"Then it's a good thing I am a good reader," Joseph responded. The two men walked away together, leaving the women to get acquainted.

"I must tell you, Mary," Elizabeth began, "that the instant I saw you, the babe in my womb leaped for joy and I was wonderfully warmed! You have been blessed by the Lord above all other women."

"What wonderful thing has happened in this house?" Mary asked.

"I, too, am expecting a miracle," Elizabeth told her. "My womb was so long barren and I did not believe that I would ever be blessed with child. But what a privilege I am to have, to bear the one who will go before the Messiah and make ready for His kingdom.

Elizabeth continued, "When the babe leaped in me, I knew that your babe is the Promised One of Israel and my son was rejoicing." Now Mary knew for sure that her vision of the angel was real!

"I am amazed," Mary said, "at the wonders our God is doing – how He has arranged that we could be together and that you would know my wonderful secret, for I have told no one but Mother and she didn't believe me."

"Then we shall let God reveal it in His time," Elizabeth assured her.

Elizabeth took Mary to the room she was to have and left her to rest before they all met again for the evening meal. Mary's heart was overflowing with joy! She would be the mother of the Messiah! She couldn't contain her emotions any longer and burst into song, praising God.

Joseph had returned to Nazareth the next morning. He would keep busy with the work he knew would be waiting for him. He would try to get it caught up before it was time for him to return to Kir Jarim to bring Mary home after Elizabeth's baby was born.

The days passed along blissfully the next three months for Mary and Elizabeth. They chatted as old friends do as they went about usual tasks during the days. Their mutual pregnancies were often the topic when they were alone. Mary asked many questions and Elizabeth was delighted to answer them according to her experience so far. One day in the courtyard, Zacharias called Elizabeth aside and wrote on his tablet, "Hasn't Mary gained weight since she has been with us? I didn't think she was eating too much."

With a sly look and a wave of the hand telling him to wait a minute, she sought out Mary. A quick conversation with her and two smiling women returned to him.

"I am not gaining weight, sir," Mary said.

"She is having a baby!" Elizabeth said. "And He is the Messiah!"

"How can you know this?" wrote the puzzled Zacharias.

"When first I saw Mary, my babe leaped in my womb," answered Elizabeth.

"And I received the news from an angel," Mary added.

The stunned Zacharias sat down on a bench while he absorbed what they were telling him.

"Why didn't Joseph say something to me?" he wrote.

"Because he doesn't know," Mary answered. "The angel said that he would know at the right time, so I shouldn't worry bout it."

"So we will let God reveal it in His time," Zacharias wrote. Things seemed to make even more sense to him now that he knew about Mary. These two women were the embodiment of God's power and providence for His chosen people. He searched again in the Scripture, seeking all the prophecies about the coming of the Messiah and also the return of the prophet Elijah who would proclaim the Messiah to the world. He became increasingly convinced that his son, who the angel had instructed him to name John, meaning "God has been gracious", was "The voice of one crying in the wilderness: Prepare the way of the Lord" prophesied by Isaiah – he who would announce the Messiah! If only he could speak!

Mary was awakened by the servant, who excitedly told her, "Hurry, the mistress is birthing the baby."

It was still early, but as she quickly dressed, Mary heard another voice and knew that it was the midwife Zacharias had hired for this occasion. Elizabeth uttered a half moan, half scream as Mary entered the room. Childbirth must be terribly painful, Mary thought as she paused at the doorway, for she knew what a strong woman Elizabeth was. And yet, as she stepped into the room, she saw a smile on Elizabeth's face. She seemed to be exulting in the task of bringing God's gift to her and Zacharias into the world.

The midwife allowed her to rest a minute or two and then urged her to push again. In three more pushes the baby's head emerged and the midwife deftly guided the shoulders through the opening. She was soon holding a slippery new baby in her hands. The servant girl laid a cloth next to her. She laid the child on it and began to wipe the birth debris from its face and nostrils. When she cleared his mouth, he gave a hearty, robust cry. There was joy in the air both in the room and below, where the friends who had joined Zacharias in his vigil were waiting in the courtyard.

As the midwife laid the precious bundle of her newborn son in Elizabeth's arms, Mary thought she saw the glory of God on her face. She was radiant. She didn't look tired, though Mary knew that she must be. Then Zacharias entered the room and his eyes glistened with tears of unexplainable joy. The promise sent to him through the angel had become a reality! How he wanted to praise God! He could not speak, but he could praise God in his silence, so after kissing his new son, Zacharias went into his prayer closet.

There was much to do for the new baby. The servant girl was kept busy washing out the soiled linens and clothes. It seemed like he spent as much time needing to eat and be cleaned up as he did sleeping. And, of course, his parents and Mary wanted to hold him a great deal, too. And there were the many visitors who came to see Elizabeth and Zacharias' miracle child. Gradually, the household settled into a kind of routine and became very comfortable.

When the baby was eight days old, he was taken to the synagogue to be presented to God and for circumcision, the sign of God's covenant with His people. It was a momentous occasion and the entire household accompanied them. When Zacharias held the child out to the priest, he was asked, "What is the name of this child?"

Elizabeth spoke and said, "John, his name is John."

Immediately, there were voices of protest all about them.

"There is no one in your family named John."

"Don't you mean Zacharias?"

"Where did 'John' come from?"

"Surely you meant Zacharias!"

Suddenly, in a strong voice, Zacharias opened his mouth and said. "His name is John." Everyone gasped and looked at the long-mute man. He spoke for the first time in more than nine months.

"His name is John," he repeated.

Everyone was thrilled that Zacharias was once again speaking and giving his account of the events that began in the Temple with the angel's announcement and culminated in this baby's birth. Now he could praise God aloud.

He raised his voice and prophesied, "Blessed is the Lord God of Israel, for He has visited and redeemed His people, and has raised up a horn of salvation for us in the house of His servant David." He continued talking, but Mary noted that he had said that the redeemer was from the house of David. Zacharias was a Levite, not a Judean. Was he talking about her baby? Her pregnancy was beginning to show, but others were not made aware of it. She listened again.

"You, child, will be called the prophet of the Highest; for you will go before the face of the Lord to prepare His ways, to give knowledge of salvation to His people by the remission of their sins," he continued.

No, she decided, this song of praise was for his child, but again it reaffirmed the angel's message about her son, too.

Now that Elizabeth's time had been fulfilled, Mary knew that she must soon return to Nazareth. While she was eager to return home, she knew that many questions would have to be addressed regarding her condition. How could she answer them? What would be her defense against the inevitable charge of infidelity? What would Joseph do? Who in Nazareth would believe her story about the angel's visit and accept that this child was truly the Son of God? She would have to rely on God's guidance to help her through this problem, but perhaps Elizabeth and Zacharias could also help her.

Joseph's Story

It was a long walk back to Nazareth alone. When Mary had been with him on the walk to Kir Jarim, it hadn't seemed nearly so long. The more he was around Mary, the more anxious he was to finalize their marriage. This interruption to their plans would only prolong the sweet agony of anticipation. He had known that she would be the best choice for his wife since he had first noticed her that day by the well. She had not yet come into her womanhood, but as she lifted her water jar to her head and started walking toward her home, he had been filled with a desire to know her better.

He began to watch for her through the window of his carpentry shop as she would go to and from the well daily. Occasionally, his attention had been caught by a lyrical laugh outside and he would see Mary dart past, usually followed by one of her brothers. The laugh turned into a ripple and he knew that the brother had caught her. She seemed so full of a joy that he longed to bring into his life.

One day his mother, Sarah, had caught him gazing at Mary and remarked, "She is nearing the time when someone will ask for her, isn't she?"

Joseph had blushed as he turned to his mother and answered, "And who do you think it will be?"

"It could be you," she replied, adding, "but you shouldn't wait too long."

Joseph thought about this. He was well-established as a carpenter. He had a good reputation for the fine work that he turned out. His prices were fair and he always had plenty of work to do. He was at the right age – not too young and not too old – to begin a family. With God's blessing, there would be many children if he started soon.

Suddenly, he put down his tools and told Sarah that he would return shortly.

As he walked toward Mary's house, he rehearsed what he would say to her father. Somehow, the words just didn't seem to be right. He stopped under a cedar tree to think it through. The fragrance of the tree seemed to soothe his apprehensions and soon he knew what to say.

As he was nearing the house, he saw Mary combing the flax for her mother. She looked like the picture of domesticity and his resolve was doubled. He strode right past her without a word and when he reached the doorway, he called out to her mother.

"Hail, I would speak with Esau, the head of this house. Is he here?"

"I am here," Esau called back, "come in."

When Joseph entered the house, he saw Esau on a mat in the corner. Beside him was a crude stick, with which he began lifting himself up to greet his guest.

"I was not aware that you were injured," Joseph remarked.

"A ram charged me yesterday and I tripped over a small boulder, wrenching my leg," Esau explained. "It should be well with a few days rest. What did you come to speak with me about?"

"I am not a man to beat about the bush," Joseph began, "so I will ask you straight out for the hand of Mary."

"You are asking to marry our little Mary?" Esau asked. "She is still a child."

"I find her to be of the betrothal age and ask that you consider my proposal," Joseph continued. "I have a fine business with as much work as I can do. It provides me with a comfortable living and I have a house which I would like to fill with your grandchildren."

Esau stroked his beard thoughtfully. "You do not address the question of her dowry."

"How soon do you think she will be of age?" Joseph queried.

"Perhaps in another year," Esau replied.

"At that time would you accept my proposal?" pressed Joseph.

"If the bride price is right, I would consider it," Esau answered.

"I will tell you what the price is when I receive your commitment to the union," Joseph countered.

"If you return in a year, I will consider your proposal," Esau conceded.

Having received an affirmative answer, Joseph returned to his shop and told his mother that he had a promise from Mary's father to consider his proposal for Mary in one year. "Humph!" was her response. "Hold his feet to the fire on that one," she counseled.

Patiently, Joseph had waited the year agreed upon and finally, the day came. With a feeling of elation, he strode over to the house of Esau.

"I would have a word with Esau, the father of Mary," he called out.

"And what would the word be?" Esau asked as he came to meet Joseph.

"I am come to accept your blessing upon the betrothal of your daughter Mary to me," came the reply.

Esau looked at the ground and stroked his beard. "I have not heard what you offer for her," he muttered.

"Mary is worth a king's ransom to me," Joseph began, "I offer twenty gold coins and a fine chest in which Anne can store many things."

"That doesn't sound like a 'king's ransom' to me," Esau observed.

"What else would you add if you were in my position?" Joseph asked.

After what seemed to Joseph to be an eternity, he looked up and told him "I do not care so much about the size of the brideprice. If she is worth more to you than what you have offered, you may add to it. When you are satisfied with your offer, I will know how much you want her for your wife. How much is that?"

Esau turned and walked away a few steps. Turning, he gave Joseph a sideways look.

"I want her with all my heart," Joseph replied, "I have loved her since she was a child and will provide a comfortable home filled with whatever she needs, children and love." The answer seemed to please Esau. He smiled and walked back to where Joseph was standing. He extended his hand, saying, "I give to you my blessing."

Eagerly, Joseph grasped his hand. Esau put his other arm around Joseph's shoulders and together they walked inside to tell the women of the betrothal.

The news had delighted Joseph's mother. Sarah had already come to love Mary's sweet nature and cheerful ways. She had observed her carefully during the past year, knowing of Joseph's desire to take her for his wife. Sarah was sure that she would be quick to learn the tasks that would be expected of her in this new role and that she would keep a lively household for her son.

Anticipating that Esau would honor his request for Mary's hand on the day the year was up, Joseph and Sarah together with Abram, Joseph's closest friend, had already made preparations for the betrothal celebration to be held the following week. It was a grand affair by the local standards and everyone in the village had attended. There was a great feast with much wine and special delicacies and dancing. Then the ceremony in which Joseph gave Mary a ring symbolizing the troth. The merriment continued well into the night and the following day.

Mary came to Joseph's house early the next morning to begin her duties as a betrothed woman.

Sarah noticed the eagerness Mary showed as she greeted her.

"I could hardly sleep last night," Mary exclaimed.

"You are eager to begin?" Sarah posed.

"I want to be the best wife a man ever had," she responded.

"Good, we shall begin with the most important part of your household duties, one which you must tend to before anything else – the food you place before your husband," Sarah told her. "You should know that all other things that come up in a marriage are more easily forgiven if the man has a stomach which is satisfied with tasty food. Come and I will show you all of Joseph's favorite foods."

As Sarah had expected, Mary quickly became adept at the tasks shown to her. In addition to her eagerness to learn, she was good company.

"Did you help your mother prepare food?" Sarah asked.

"I helped with some things, but I never prepared an entire meal for us," Mary responded. "I got the water and kneaded the dough for bread, but I really don't know what all Mother does. She is a good model, but not much of a teacher, I'm afraid."

"Sometimes we get so busy doing the necessary tasks, that we forget to pass our knowledge on to others. But maybe she didn't want to teach you too much so that when you learned about how to do for your own husband from his mother, you would not have to remember to change things," Sarah offered.

"I'm sure that was her thought," Mary agreed, "and I'm so glad to have such a good teacher to show me the proper way for Joseph. I look forward to the day we will set up our own home. Will we begin here with you?"

"Perhaps, in the beginning, but probably not for long," Sarah said.

"I shall always cherish any time I can spend with you," stated Mary.

The two women chatted amiably as meals were prepared, clothes were washed and house was kept and Mary gained much wisdom about every day married life from her mother-in-law.

Several months had passed when Anne and Esau came with Mary to meet with Joseph and Sarah to discuss the letter which Anne had received from her cousin's husband, a priest at the Jerusalem temple. The woman, who was a little older than Anne, was now nearing the sixth month of her confinement and her husband wanted a family member to be with her until after the baby's birth. He asked if Anne's daughter, Mary, would be able to come for the final part of the pregnancy and the early days of the baby's life.

Esau started the discussion, asking, "Mary is your betrothed, Joseph. What do you think?"

"She still has a great deal to learn from Mother and I don't want to put off the wedding for a long period of time. I don't want her to go," he answered.

"But, she has already learned the most important duties in keeping a house," Sarah said. Then, turning to Anne, she asked, "Mary is the youngest in your family. Has she ever cared for babies or witnessed childbirth?"

"No," Anne answered, "as far as I know, she has had very little contact with babies or even young children."

"I didn't think about that," Joseph added. "This would be a chance for her to learn about babies. I hope to have many children, so she would need to know how to care for them. Maybe she should go."

"Yes, son," agreed Sarah, "she really needs to have this knowledge to be a good wife to you. She has already learned so much from me about keeping house that she could easily do a fine job of it."

Anne interjected, "I know that both of you would miss each other terribly, but it would only be for a season and that will not seem so long as your family grows."

"I'll miss her, too," added Esau, "but this experience would undoubtedly make my little Mary a much better mother. Is it then agreed that she should go?"

It was decided that Joseph would take Mary to Anne's cousin's home where she would remain until the child was a month or two old so that she could take part in his care. On her return to Nazareth, the wedding would take place. And so, the betrothed couple had made the journey.

Joseph had to work very hard during the time of Mary's absence in order to finish all of the work he had, because he knew more would accumulate while he was gone. One good thing was that he would have some extra money for them to start their marriage.

Time was passing more quickly than he had thought it would, probably because he was working frantically to keep up with the work, which seemed to be much heavier than usual. It was like everyone in the village needed something made. Joseph was working from dawn to dusk every day but the Sabbath. How glad he was that God, in His infinite wisdom, had ordained a day of rest every week!

Joseph saw the crowd gathering in the marketplace. He laid his tools down and joined them. The Roman soldier turned from nailing the notice to the post, mounted his horse and made his way out of the gathering people. Ezekiel, the local priest, went to the post and read aloud,

"To all the people of Israel and its outlying provinces,

"By order of Caesar Augustus, Emperor of Rome

"It is hereby decreed that everyone without exception shall be counted. Every person must return to the city of the origin of his line and be registered by a Roman official no later than the autumnal equinox. Failure or refusal to obey this order will bring immediate death."

As soon as Ezekiel finished reading the notice, there was a mad scurry as each one rushed home to tell their family and others about the edict of the emperor.

Sarah, hearing the flurry of activity came to the door as Joseph approached.

"The Roman emperor has ordered everyone to go to the town of their lineage and be counted. It must be done within the month," he told his mother.

"But what about Mary," she asked. "You were to go next week to bring her home."

"I know, Mother, let's think about what can be done. Right now, I've got to get busy and finish my work. We'll talk more later."

After the evening meal, Sarah and Joseph sat down near the fire. Joseph looked again at the letter from Elizabeth saying that her baby was doing well and that Mary was ready to come home.

"I had planned on leaving the day after Sabbath to bring her home, but now I may have to go to be registered instead," he said. Joseph was of the line of David, whose home had been Bethlehem. "Of course, it would not be as far to take Mary on to Bethlehem with me before bringing her back to Nazareth," he mused aloud.

"No," added Sarah, "and she would probably like to have that much extra time with you alone after so long a separation."

So it was decided that Joseph would go to Kir Jarim, then on to Bethlehem. He sent word that he would come to get her in a week and then he doubled his efforts to complete the work awaiting him.

Joseph's steps quickened more as he neared Kir Jiram for he knew that he would soon see Mary again. He had missed her more than he had expected. She had been such a presence in his home as she learned from his mother all she would need to know to make a good wife for him. Her cheerful spirit and playful conversation added a liveliness that he treasured. He wished that they didn't have to wait until they returned to Nazareth to consummate their union, but his mother and Mary's parents would insist that the ceremony take place there so they could be part of it.

Impatiently, Joseph knocked on the door of Zacharias and Elizabeth's home. It seemed like an hour before the servant girl opened it. When she saw Joseph, she smiled broadly and turned on her heel running through the courtyard shouting, "He's here, Mary. He's here." Joseph, left standing at the door, came inside and closed it. When he turned around, there she was – his Mary.

As she walked toward him, he noticed something different about her. Her gait was not the same graceful step she had when he left her here. He looked more closely and saw that she was not wearing her usual sash around her waist. He couldn't believe his eyes when he saw the bulge beneath her tunic. It can't be, he thought. I haven't been with her and I know that she would never be unfaithful to me, but the bulge is unmistakable. She is heavy with child!

The smile on Mary's face faded as she read the dark thoughts Joseph was thinking. How could she explain this situation to him? The two of them stood there looking at each other, unable to say a word.

"Joseph!" Elizabeth cried as she and Zacharias entered the courtyard. They crossed the open space with their arms wide and embraced the stunned man. Still Joseph said nothing.

"How happy we are to see you," she continued, "Mary has taken such good care of us and we have taken good care of Mary."

"How can you say that," stammered Joseph. "Look at her!"

"Yes, doesn't she look wonderful? You are so fortunate," answered Zacharias. Suddenly he realized what Joseph was thinking? Turning to Mary, he asked, "You didn't tell him your wonderful news?"

Mary bowed her head and said softly, "I don't know how to."

"Goodness," Zacharias responded, "no wonder he is surprised."

Although all three of them tried to tell Joseph about Mary's pregnancy, he only seemed to get more confused. His mind was filled with terrible accusations which drowned out the words of the others. Finally, Zacharias suggested that he go to bed and they would try to make things more sensible to him the next day. Joseph agreed that he needed some time alone to think things out. His world was totally shattered.

After refusing to eat, he told them that he would like to make a pallet of straw in the courtyard for the night. He laid a bed of straw and spread his mantle on it. Wearily he sat in the middle of it. He buried his head in his hands and wept. He had to think this through, but all he could think of was that he was losing Mary. How could such a horrible thing have happened? He didn't understand the things that Zacharias and Elizabeth and Mary had told him. It didn't make sense at all. The fact was that Mary was pregnant and would soon bear a child that was not his.

According to the law, he could cast her out publicly and she would pay for her deception by living the rest of her life as an outcast, probably turning to prostitution in order to stay alive. Or he could give her a bill of divorcement and send her on her way. A man did not need any real reason to divorce his wife and even though they were only betrothed, they were still considered to be married. But how would he be able to explain his action to Mary's parents? Maybe they already knew about it and were trying to trap him into a marriage to save face for their daughter. Maybe this whole thing about Elizabeth's baby had been part of a plot.

Looking toward the heavens with his arms upraised, Joseph cried out in a loud voice, "My God, help me!" The other occupants heard him, but left him to his solitude. Mary cried softly for she knew the anguish he was suffering, but she resolved to leave it in God's hands, remembering the angel's words, "He will know when the time is right."

Joseph lay down and tried to sleep, but the problem kept nagging him. Finally, he knew what he must do. He loved Mary and did not want to hurt her, so he would write out the bill of divorcement tomorrow morning before he left and she would still be in a safe place until she could make other living arrangements. He would go on his way to Bethlehem alone. Resigned, he sighed as the weariness of the road finally overtook him. His fitful sleep was interrupted by a bright light. He tried to ignore it, but a voice said, "Do not be afraid, Joseph, to take Mary for your wife for that which is conceived in her is of the Holy Spirit. She will give birth to a Son and you shall name Him Jesus, for He will save His people from their sins."

As he opened his eyes and sat up, he saw a man clothed in white linen and surrounded by a dazzling light. Just as suddenly as it had come, the vision was gone.

Joseph rubbed his eyes. Had it been real? Was he dreaming or had God sent him a vision or one of his angels? His mind started sorting through the things Mary, Elizabeth and Zacharias had said to him. Slowly, he became convinced that he *had* seen an angel and now he believed. If this baby was truly to be the Son of God, he, Joseph, was highly privileged to be chosen to be the temporal father of the Messiah. The longer he pondered this thought, the more overwhelming the responsibility became. He had never been a father before and now he would be an earthly father to God's Son? Would the boy be perfect or would He need to be taught right from wrong and disciplined as other boys were? How would one discipline the Son of God? How would one be a father to someone who was perfect? How could he even think of being such a person?

Joseph prostrated himself and again cried out to God for His help. He would do his best, but he knew that without God's help, he wasn't up to the task. Even though he spent the rest of the night praying, he arose rested with the sun as the household again came to life.

Seeing the servant girl scurry across the courtyard as she took an armful of wood for the early morning fire, he called to her.

"Is Mary awake?" he asked.

"Yes, sir, would you like me to get her for you?"

"Please."

Soon Mary came down the steps from the living quarters. She looked different this morning, Joseph thought. Or was he just seeing her through enlightened eyes. He smiled and Mary came to him. He opened wide his arms and embraced his betrothed.

"I'm so sorry that I doubted you, Mary," he whispered in her ear. "I know that you could never have betrayed me. You are the sweetest, purest girl I have ever known and I love you." Tears ran down Mary's face as she realized that the angel had finally told Joseph her wonderful secret.

Elizabeth and Zacharias came down the steps and saw the pair. Tears of joy flowed from their eyes as they saw the couple in an embrace for they knew that Joseph now would not forsake Mary. As they approached, Joseph opened his arms and the two faced them.

"Thank you both for the part you have played in keeping my Mary safe during this time," he began. "Last night I received a messenger from the Lord and know that what you were telling me is the truth. I am most honored to be chosen to be the earthly father to God's Son."

"Praise God," rejoiced Elizabeth.

Zacharias added, "I would be honored if you would allow me to perform the marriage ceremony for you before you go to Bethlehem." When Joseph saw the joy on Mary's face, he accepted the offer. Their family in Nazareth would just have to accept it, too.

The wedding was very simple, but fulfilled all the requirements of the Law. The couple regretted that their family could not join with them in this celebration, but they were comforted by the thought that the most important member of the family, God, was there in their midst.

Following the ritual, Joseph and Zacharias went to find a friend from whom Joseph could buy a donkey and cart in which Mary could ride to Bethlehem. They would continue the journey the following morning. That night Mary and Joseph lay together for the first time. It was such a comfort to feel her warmth as she laid her head on his arm. He bent his neck, kissed the top of her head and drew her even closer. They were joined together at last, although he knew that he would not completely experience the marriage bed until after the baby had been born.

The day's journey had taken longer than it should have because Joseph insisted that they take many rests along the way. When they finally arrived at Bethlehem, things didn't look like they would find lodging. The village was teeming with travelers who had also come to register for the census. There were only a few inns in the area. They stopped at each one, but they were all full.

At the door of the last inn, as Joseph was talking to the innkeeper, Mary let out a long low moan. The man looked beyond Joseph and saw that the young woman was in obvious distress. Being a kind man who really wanted to help, he suggested to Joseph that if he wanted to, he could stay in the cave below the inn where he allowed his guests to keep their animals together with his own cow and goats. One quick glance back at Mary convinced Joseph that he needed to grasp this opportunity.

As they approached the cave, they could hear the animal sounds and felt a special comfort in their closeness. Inside, there was a plentiful supply of fresh straw and an empty feed trough which could serve as the baby's first bed near the entrance. Joseph helped Mary down from the cart and she sat on a large stone nearby. The night air was cooling rapidly, but inside the enclosure the body warmth of the animals made the temperature comfortable.

Joseph made a bed of the fresh straw on the floor next to the trough, which he also filled with straw in preparation for the new life which would soon fill it. He laid a blanket on the bed and Mary came and lay down. She was tired from the long trip and would have drifted off to sleep, but her labor had begun. Joseph hurriedly cared for the donkey and returned to Mary's side.

It was late in the night when the first cry of God's Son was heard. Joseph had not thought about getting a midwife to help Mary, so when the birth came, he attended her and with God's help, delivered the Messiah. Together the couple wrapped the Baby in tight cloths and after his mother held Him for a time, they placed Him in the manger bed. A ray of light shone on the sleeping child, drawing their attention to the brilliance of the sky which had driven away the night.

Joseph walked outside and saw that the night was even brighter than a harvest moon. Although he saw no source for the extraordinary light, he knew in his heart that this was another of God's affirmations of the arrival of His Son and the beginning of His earthly journey. He bowed down and worshiped God, giving thanks for this miraculous event and for allowing him to be a part of it. He asked for God's guidance in everything that he would do from this time on throughout the rest of his life, that he might be a proper father.

Joseph was resting next to Mary and they had both just dozed off when they were awakened by the sounds of walking feet, hushed voices and bleating sheep. He arose and as he reached the entrance he saw a large group of people and sheep coming down the slope from the street above, where the inn was located. He stared in amazement as the number grew and grew. The whole scene was brilliantly illuminated. Soon the entire meadow was filled with townspeople, mingled with shepherds and their flocks.

He looked back and saw that Mary, too, had awakened and was now leaning over to the trough. She picked the baby up and held Him close to her. Joseph approached the crowd. Several of the shepherds came to meet him. In excited voices they addressed him.

"Was this baby born tonight?"

"The angels announced his birth to us."

"They came in a blaze of light."

"The angels said that this baby is the savior God has promised to Israel. Is he?"

"We came to worship him."

Joseph looked around at the people. They were looking at the baby and murmuring. The shepherds had told the townspeople who had joined their procession, of the angels' announcement and the villagers wanted to see for themselves. The sheep had followed their masters, who had begun to kneel and bow their heads in worship. They had believed the vision and, apparently, so did the others as they, too, began to kneel.

Joseph walked back to Mary's side and quickly told her what he had been told and what he had seen. She looked down at the child in her arms and smiled. Then she looked at the crowd and marveled that God had brought so many witnesses to the birth of His Son. She and Joseph had talked that day as they traveled along.

"Mother and father will be so sorry that they did not attend our wedding," Mary said. "I am their only daughter."

"My mother will also be disappointed when she learns of it, but it would appear that this was God's will," he replied.

"I did not know how to make them understand about the baby's soon birth."

"It would have been impossible to explain," Joseph agreed.

"If we follow God's guidance in our lives, He will protect His Son and us."

"No matter what we are told to do, we must not ever question God's instructions, but always obey immediately.

"The rest of our lives we must live according to God and He will see us through whatever we face," Mary affirmed, adding, "He will always show us the way and provide for our needs."

Now Mary and Joseph looked out at the vast crowd kneeling before them in prayers of thanksgiving for the privilege of witnessing the appearance of the child who had been proclaimed by angels as Messiah. Joseph and Mary knew that because of this baby, they were now kin to multitudes of people.

Gradually the crowd thinned out and as the shepherds left, so did their flocks. Soon there was only one couple left. The woman held a young child on her shoulder. As her husband knelt and prayed, she bowed her head in prayer. Then they, too, returned to their home leaving Mary and Joseph once again marveling at their new charge.

Home

Joseph awoke as the sun was beginning to crest the hill across the valley. He smiled as he looked at Mary, sleeping so peacefully. Perhaps he could go and get in line early for the registration. If so, he would not have to wait so long, he thought. Hurriedly he arranged things so that Mary would not have to move too much to care for the baby, who was also sleeping. As he gave her a tender kiss, Mary's eyes opened. Joseph quickly told her what he was doing and that he would have the innkeeper send something for her to eat and drink, then he left.

The innkeeper knew that the baby had been born as he, too, was in the crowd of onlookers and was more than happy to provide nourishment for the young mother. A short time after Joseph's departure the innkeeper's young daughter brought a basket with freshly baked bread, dates, nuts and some goat's milk to the stable for Mary. Together, they admired the beautiful new child.

Joseph found that the line was only about ten men long when he got in it. The topic of discussion was the brilliant light and the procession of shepherds through the town during the night.

"What was all the commotion last night? Do the shepherds always bring their flocks through the town at night in Bethlehem?" one asked.

"And did you see how bright the moon was last night? It wasn't time for the full moon. What do you think it was?" another added.

"I live here and the answer to your question is No. The shepherds don't bring their flocks into town at night, only to the edge of town on market day," a third stated.

"Did you see anything?" the first man asked Joseph, drawing him into the conversation.

"My wife and I only arrived last night and she gave birth during the night, so I was too busy helping her…" Joseph began.

"Didn't you have a midwife for her?" interrupted the man.

"I didn't have time to find one," Joseph replied, "Her labor began while we were still on the road."

"Where are you staying? Are you at an inn or at someone's house?" queried one.

"The only place in town was the inn's stable," Joseph answered.

"That's no place for a new baby," exclaimed the man who had said that he lived here. "My name is Jonas and I have a place where you can stay. My mother died last year and her house is at the edge of town. It has fallen into disrepair, but if you want to fix the roof so that it doesn't leak, you're welcome to use it for the time you are here."

Joseph thanked him for the offer and told him that they could go see the place when they were registered. Jonas moved back in the line so that he could talk more with Joseph.

Jonas asked, "Are you planning on staying here a little longer to give your wife a chance to rest from the labor?"

Joseph hadn't thought ahead that far. Surely, Mary would need to rest. Even if he completed the registration today, they shouldn't leave so soon. And then, if they tarried longer in Bethlehem, they wouldn't have so far to go to the Temple for Mary's purification thirty-three days after the baby's delivery.

"I hadn't thought about that, but you are right. She should rest a bit," he answered.

"Where are you from?" asked Jonas.

"I am a carpenter in Nazareth of Galilee."

"Have you lived there long?"

"All of my life, but my father came from Bethlehem before I was born. His name is Jacob. He is the son of Matthan, the son of Eleazer. My great grandfather, Eleazer, was a carpenter here in Bethlehem, which is why we are here registering," Joseph answered.

"I am also a great grandson of Eleazer the carpenter. That makes us family," Jonas delightedly said, offering his hand as if to seal the connection. "My house is a good house. Perhaps you would want to make this your home. There is much work for a good carpenter here."

"Let us go to see the house when we finish here," replied Joseph, smiling broadly at his newfound cousin and his generous offer.

The registrars arrived and in a couple of hours both men had been registered.

As they turned from the tables, Joseph turned to Jonas.

"Before we go to see your house," he said, "I need to look in on my wife, Mary, and see if she needs anything."

"I would like to go with you, if you don't mind," Jonas eagerly offered. "I live at the far end of town and did not hear the sounds last night."

"Of course," Joseph answered, "I would like for you to meet Mary."

Together, the two men walked down the slope to the cave. As they approached, they saw the innkeeper's daughter and wife with Mary. When the girl had come to bring something for Mary to eat and to milk the cow, she found that the baby had been born. She hurried back and told her mother, who joined her when she returned, bringing some cloths and other things Mary would need for the baby's care. The girl had gone to her milking while her mother and Mary talked about the baby.

When Joseph and Jonas entered the cave, the innkeeper's wife and daughter left.

"Mary," he began, "meet Jonas, who is my cousin. This is my new son."

"You have a fine son, Joseph," Jonas stated, adding, "I told Joseph that you would need to rest at least a few days. I have an empty house nearby and would be pleased to have you stay there as long as you would care to."

Mary smiled and answered, "What a generous and thoughtful offer. It would be good to have a more comfortable place for our son to begin his life. Thank you."

"Do you have everything you need?" asked Joseph.

"Yes," Mary replied. "We are both doing very well."

"Then I will go and see the house with Jonas. I won't be gone long," Joseph told her as the two men left.

The house was fairly large, Joseph discovered. It had two rooms and an extended roof which would provide shelter for the donkey and a place where he could set up a carpenter shop if they decided to stay for a while. The roof had a few places where it would leak in a rain, but that would be easy for Joseph to repair. There were still a few pieces of furniture in it. A stool, a table and a reed box which they could use to store their belongings. It would do nicely and Jonas didn't want them to pay him at all for its use. "As long as you need it," Jonas had emphasized.

Mary was both delighted and relieved by Jonas' offer. That such a place was available to them was an answer to a prayer. As she had prepared things to be placed on the donkey for transport to their new home, she thought about the way God was taking care of them. He had caused things to work out so that she would not have to go home with her obvious pregnancy to explain. He had made His will clear to Joseph and had arranged their wedding. He had provided a calm place in which she could give birth and now He had provided a home for her little family.

Joseph placed the bundles Mary had packed on the donkey and she picked up her most precious bundle out of the manger. Looking around one more time, she bid a silent goodbye to the unusual birthplace and she, Joseph and the donkey walked up the slope.

Rachel had been curious when she saw Jonas and another man looking at the house across the street. She wondered if he was going to sell or rent it. He hadn't even been to it since his mother died. She saw the two men shake hands and leave.

It was less than an hour later when she saw the man return to the house, leading a laden donkey and his wife who was holding a baby. Looking closer, Rachel realized that they were the people she and Eli had seen last night in the stable-cave. Could it be possible that they were moving into the house across the street? Were they to be neighbors? Could it be that the baby was the Son of God as the shepherds had claimed last night? It seemed to Rachel that her life was always full of questions. She felt like she was forever looking for an answer.

She picked Jacob up and went across the street to welcome the couple. She was anxious to have a chance to talk to them. She hoped that they were going to stay more than a few days. It would be nice to have someone to talk with and the woman looked so very young, perhaps she, too, would like to have someone to talk to. It was obvious that they were far from home and alone.

"I bid you welcome," she said as she neared the house. "My name is Rachel and this is my son, Jacob."

Mary turned to face Rachel and smiled. "My name is Mary and this is my newborn." There was a radiance about her that Rachel attributed to her new son.

"You spent last night in the inn's stable, didn't you?" she asked.

"Yes," Mary replied, "we found no other place and I had begun my labor. Actually it was a comforting place to be. The warmth created by the animals and their quiet movements made me feel not so alone."

"We were among those who came last night and saw you all," Rachel said. "The shepherds were saying that God had announced to them the birth of His Son in Bethlehem. They were convinced that He is your baby. Is he?"

"What do you think?" Mary asked. She studied Rachel. What would she do if she knew Mary's secret knowledge? Then she decided that God had revealed this news to those He chose and she would let Him answer Rachel's question in His time and way.

"All I know was that last night was one which I shall never forget," Rachel stated. "The brilliance of the night. The shepherds. Everyone kneeling in worship as if the baby *was* the Son of God," she continued. "I shall always remember it."

Joseph came around the corner of the house carrying some of the bundles from the donkey, which he had tied in the stable/carpenter shop behind the house. Mary called to him.

"Joseph, come and meet our neighbor, Rachel."

"I'm so happy to see that you are moving into this house," Rachel said.

"We are grateful to my cousin for offering his house to us," he replied. "It will be good to know that you live so close to us."

"I had better go inside and see what needs to be done," said Mary.

"Do you need anything?" asked Rachel.

"A broom if you have one," answered Joseph as he came out of the house on the way to get another load.

Mary carried the baby into the house. She was happy to see that there were two rooms. It was much bigger than she had expected. There were a few pieces of furniture, but nowhere to lay the baby while she worked at cleaning the place up. Rachel appeared at the door with a broom in her hand. She offered to hold the baby while Mary swept out a corner in which to lay him.

Joseph had brought in all the belongings from the donkey and disappeared. Soon he was back and the women heard sounds coming from the back of the house. Mary finished sweeping and traded Rachel the broom for the baby. Reluctantly, Rachel surrendered the precious bundle.

"What will you name your baby?" she asked.

Mary replied, "His name is to be Jesus. When is your baby to be born?"

Rachel blushed, but she was glad that Mary had asked about her wonderful expected event.

"It will be a couple of months yet," she responded. They chatted like old friends until Jacob, who had been playing at Rachel's feet, grew bored and decided that it was time to go home. He tugged at his mother's tunic and she picked him up, said her goodbyes to Mary and Joseph and returned to her home to prepare for Eli's evening meal.

As she left, she thought, he is such a beautiful baby, every bit as beautiful as my Jacob. It would be wonderful to have these people for neighbors.

By time for the evening meal, Joseph had produced a simple cradle in which Mary could put the baby while he slept and she tended to the work necessary to set up housekeeping. He had also gone to the market and purchased two jars, one for water and the other for baking. He filled the water jar on his way back to the house. He gathered grass and small sticks for the fire in the baking jar and, late in the afternoon, bought the necessary items for grinding wheat and making bread, as well as a supply of dates, nuts and lentils at the market and some bread from the baker's shop to eat today.

Mary and Joseph were tired after their brief rest the night before and their busy, eventful day, so when Eli came to their door in the early evening with a big load of fresh straw for their bed, they were very grateful.

"I am Eli, Rachel's husband," he said. "Rachel came to me in the field and told me of our new neighbors. She had suggested that you could use straw for a bed."

"We sure can!" replied Joseph. "Thank you for thinking about it. Can I pay you for it?"

"No, please consider it a gift to a new friend."

"I am Joseph. It is good to have a friend any time, but especially now. Can you come in and meet my wife, Mary?"

"I'm sorry. My wife is expecting me for our meal, but I will talk more with you tomorrow. Sleep well," Eli said as he turned toward the door.

After they ate their evening meal, Mary had hardly spread the blanket over the straw when Joseph lay on it and pronounced it good. She nursed the baby, then joined him and God blessed them all with a sound and well-earned rest.

On the eighth day after the baby's birth, Joseph and Mary brought Him to the synagogue for his circumcision. The rabbi took the child and as he performed the ritual, he spoke. "Blessed be the Lord our God, who has sanctified us by His precepts and given us circumcision."

Joseph responded, "Who has sanctified us by His precepts and has granted us to introduce our child into the covenant of Abraham our father."

"What name do you give the child?" the priest asked.

"His name is Jesus," answered Joseph.

As the days passed and it grew nearer to the day of their trip to the Temple in Jerusalem for Mary's purification and the dedication of the baby, Mary and Joseph discussed their plans. Joseph had quickly found that there was ample work available in Bethlehem as Jonas had been spreading the word about his skill as a carpenter and he was being approached to do work by a number of people. Having left his tools in Nazareth, he had to get more, either by buying them or making them, but he could do it in a short time. He had already collected enough to get started, in order to repair the roof and make the cradle for his new son. For now they would stay in Bethlehem, but they would keep the donkey for a while, in case they decided to return to Nazareth.

Mary liked Rachel and Eli and felt a kinship growing between the two families. The houses were near the well and not far from the market. And she loved being able to see the open spaces of the fields outside her door. It would not be hard to live here, she thought. Perhaps this was where God wanted them to raise His Son – in the birthplace of his ancestor, King David. After all, He had provided them with a fine place to live, a way for Joseph to make a livelihood and friends to make them feel welcome. Perhaps this was God's will. They would pray about it and wait for God's affirmation or redirection.

The fall evenings were a welcome time for the young families. The crowds had disappeared as the census was completed and the village was once again peaceful and quiet in the evenings. Most of the harvest was in, so Eli had more time with his family and the new neighbors, with whom they frequently shared evening meals.

Eli was very glad that Joseph and Mary had set up housekeeping in the house so near his. Joseph had returned his gift of the straw by building a cradle for his and Rachel's expected baby. There hadn't been one for Jacob and Joseph's gift had truly delighted them. Eli had been worried that he might be in the fields when Rachel went into labor and there would be no one to help her, or watch Jacob. He knew that she and Mary were becoming close and his worries eased considerably. It was almost like they were sisters.

They had devised a plan where one of them would watch the children while the other went to the well or wherever else she needed to go. The children had taken to each other immediately. Jacob loved to make Jesus laugh. Sometimes, he could do it just by looking at Him, but at other times he would gently run his finger along Jesus' cheek. Jacob was beginning to walk now and Rachel had to watch him carefully to see that he didn't leave their home and cross the street to see Jesus when she wasn't looking.

The Temple

Before dawn on the thirty-third day following Jesus' birth, Mary and Joseph took their baby to Jerusalem for Mary's purification rites at the Temple. Mary's youth stood her in good stead as they walked the five-mile distance. She was tired by the time they reached the city, so they found a quiet place and rested for a while, giving her a chance to nurse the child and eat some dates to refresh her strength. Then they passed through the teeming streets toward the Holy Mountain on which the Temple was being built.

Their route seemed to be circuitous because the streets turned this way and that, but finally they reached the huge wall which Herod had built to enlarge and flatten the top of Mount Moriah, making it into the Temple Mount. They walked down the street running alongside the wall, which soared forty cubits high, and climbed the steps leading to the arch through which they entered Temple Mount.

The Temple was very impressive, even in the current unfinished state. It was so tall! Even the doors were taller than any of the buildings Mary and Joseph had ever seen – including the synagogue in Nazareth.

Herod was a master builder and was striving to make this edifice, when it was finished, as impressive as Solomon's Temple had been. Even though it was still under construction, the Jews could and did use it daily. It was here that the sacrifices, both required and special, were made and here one paid the temple tax of one shekel. Here baby boys were brought for presentation to the Lord. Here new mothers came for purification rites. Here Mary and Joseph came to perform their sacred duty.

They entered the Temple Mount at the rear of the Courtyard of the Gentiles. The busyness of the place surprised them. Along the wall were pens of sheep, rams and bulls which had been examined by a priest and declared unblemished and fit for sacrifice. Vendors stood beside them ready to sell them to a pilgrim or someone who didn't own flocks or the appropriate beast for the required sacrifice. The bleating of the animals mixed with the sounds of money being exchanged. It was necessary for those from different cultures to exchange their coins for the shekels required for the temple tax. As they walked along the side of the wall, Joseph and Mary saw people with all kinds of strange garments. The people of God came to the Holy Temple in Jerusalem at least once in their lives to worship.

The building itself was so immense that they felt as small and insignificant as ants. This is the house of God, no wonder I am so much in awe, Mary thought.

Joseph went to a vendor of doves and purchased two of the birds, the sacrifice required for Mary's rites.

As they approached the front entrance to the Courtyard of the Women, they encountered an old man named Simeon. Although his many years clearly showed on his face, he had a look of pure joy. In a voice which crackled with excitement, he told them,

"I have waited in this courtyard for this day many years. A number of years ago, I had a vision from God when I was praying. He promised that the Holy Ghost would sustain me until I had seen the Messiah. Today I know that my prayer and the promise of God is answered."

Simeon rose with outstretched arms. He gently lifted the baby from his mother's arms. Mary looked at Joseph and he nodded his assent.

Looking heavenward, Simeon prayed aloud, "Lord, thank You for letting Your servant die in peace, as You promised. I have now seen the salvation which You have prepared for Your people, a light to reach the Gentiles."

Tears streamed down his cheeks as he returned the child to his mother. Simeon blessed the family and added, "Listen, this child will be the fall and rising again of many in Israel, a sign which shall be spoken against and a sword that will even pierce your own heart and will reveal the thoughts of many." Then he turned and limped away.

Mary stood there absorbing what the old man had said and wondering what lay in store for the tiny babe she held. What Simeon said had again affirmed her knowledge that her son was The Messiah, but he had spoken about division, not bringing the nation together. What had he meant?

Joseph had walked on. Now he stopped, realizing that Mary was not with him. Just then Mary saw him and hurried to catch up. As they continued across the courtyard, a wizened old woman came up to them. When she was in front of them, she stopped.

"My name is Anna," she began. "I have had a revelation about the babe you hold. He is to be blessed in a mighty way by God. May I pray for him?"

Mary again looked to Joseph. He had heard of the two ancient people they were encountering and knew that Anna was a prophetess who was known for her prayers day and night. He nodded his assent and Anna began to pray loudly.

"Oh, Lord our God, we thank you for this baby. We know that He is Your gift to us – that He is come to bring redemption to all who seek it. We praise You, oh Lord, for Your mercy, Your mighty power and Your precious gift. Praise be to our God!"

Other people seemed not to give her much attention, but Joseph and Mary knew that her prayer again affirmed God's revelation to them about this miraculous baby. When the woman had returned to her continuous prayers, the family proceeded into the courtyard. Joseph walked up to the priest who received the sacrifices, handing over the two doves and Mary's cleansing ritual began.

The day was bright with sunshine, although it was now cooler. Trees were losing their leaves and Rachel was glad that Eli's work was slowing down. He was nearly done harvesting the straw now. He had told her last night that he should be through with it in two or three days. It was always nice to have his company more in the winter. There was still work to be done, but the pace was much more relaxed. Happily she hummed as she passed the shuttle back and forth through the loom.

Suddenly, it struck! The pain did not come on gradually as it had when Jacob was born. This time it was sudden and sharp. When the second one hit just as hard, she forced herself to go to the doorway.

"Mary," she called, "come quick!" She sunk to the floor. Jacob came over to her, looking very serious. His eyes went from her face, which was at the same level as his now, to her hands, which were pressing on her stomach.

"Mama hurt?" he asked.

Mary came running with Jesus in her arm. Immediately she saw the situation and called back over her shoulder, "Joseph, get the midwife! Rachel's travail has begun."

Joseph put down his tools and ran down the street to get the midwife while Mary helped Rachel to lie down. She placed Jesus in the little cradle Joseph had built for Rachel's new baby and Jacob busied himself amusing his friend.

Eli came home as dusk was settling in. Mary hailed him before he entered the house inviting him and Jacob to eat with her family. She told him that Rachel was sleeping now following the birth of his new son and that Jacob was already with Joseph and Jesus. The evening meal was ready.

Eli entered his house and saw his wife sleeping soundly with the new baby beside her. How happy he was! Eli knelt next to them. He smoothed a wisp of Rachel's hair and gently caressed her face. She smiled a contented smile, but didn't open her eyes. Then he looked at the baby beside her. That was just the way Jacob looked the first time I saw him, he thought. Thank You, Lord, for the safe birth of this child, for the neighbors You have provided for this purpose and for the abundant crop in my fields. There will be no want in my house this year, he prayed. Then he rose and went across the street to join Joseph and Mary.

Winter had come and gone. In a spirit of celebration for spring, Mary and Rachel agreed to complete their household work early in the morning this day so that they could take a little walk with the children out from the town and eat their mid-morning meal under a newly-leafed tree by a brook. Spring was always the most welcome season as the earth was reborn. The pleasant days were so anticipated during the dreary winter, that it only seemed right to have such an impromptu celebration.

The toddler and the two women, each carrying a child and a small bundle, didn't go far. The tree was beside a little-used road and the clear brook next to it babbled happily. They sat down on stones with the babies on their laps and opened their bundles. Jacob sat on his own little stone. Happily they chatted as they ate. The babies cooed as they watched the leaves moving in the light breeze. Life was so good!

That evening, the two couples put the children to sleep and sat outside their homes visiting. The women had done most of their talking in the afternoon by the brook and now were content to listen to their husbands and enjoy the fresh breeze.

"It is good," began Eli, "that the weather has been so fair this year. I have nearly finished with the seeding."

"My work has not slowed down," Joseph stated. "I have been commissioned by the richest man in Bethlehem to build a handsome bed. I told him that I have never slept in or even seen a bed, but he gave me very detailed instructions. He told me that my reputation for fine work made him confident that I would do an excellent job – that there was no other craftsman he would trust with this assignment."

"What a compliment!" Eli exclaimed.

"Mary said that she is sure I can do it well, but I'm not too sure," Joseph continued. "Such a project would seem to require more detail than I am capable of delivering."

"But," Mary interjected, "I told him to look at it as a challenge and maybe one day he would find time to make another one for us to sleep on."

Rachel pointed to the sky. "This night seems unusually bright, doesn't it? It reminds me of the night Jesus was born," she said. "It almost looks like that star is making this night even brighter than that one was."

"You're right," agreed Eli.

They looked around the area. There were shadows. Even the dirt in the street seemed to glow. There were so many stars in the sky, but one unusually large one seemed so close they could touch it. They were mesmerized by the beauty of the night.

"I have a great deal of work to do tomorrow. I promised Malachi the vinedresser that I would finish his table. We'll talk more another time," said Joseph, breaking the spell of the evening. They said their good nights and returned to their homes.

Crickets chirped loudly as they lay down to sleep. It was so peaceful in Bethlehem, Rachel thought as she laid next to Eli, nursing Reuben, her new son. And it was so good to have her family with her. Her husband provided so well for them and with the extra money they had accumulated from selling bread during the census and the bounty brought by the wheat Eli had sold, they would be able to add to their house and make it more comfortable for their growing family. She placed the now sleeping baby in his cradle and tucked the soft wool blanket around him. Soon after she lay down, she joined her family in sleep.

The Visitors

There was a special hush in the air. Even the feet of the camels made no sound on the main street of Bethlehem, giving the entourage a ghostlike appearance. There were ten camels. Richly robed men rode on several of them. Servants were mounted on the others. It was obvious from their attire that they were foreigners. The servants' camels were heavily laden with tents and supplies.

Slowly the procession passed through the town. Near the edge of the village, they turned off on a small side street and came to a stop. One of the elegant men nodded and a servant dismounted and went to the door of a house. When the door opened, a sleepy-eyed Joseph looked at the astonishing sight.

"Hail to the master of the house," began the servant. "My lords are seeking the baby who was born King of the Jews. They have been following his star." With that the servant turned and pointed to the gigantic star which seemed to be directly over the house. Joseph saw that it was the brilliant star they had noticed earlier, which was still dominating the sky.

"Who might these lords be?" he asked.

"They are wise men from the East. They have traveled for many months following the star and they wish to pay homage to this child," was the reply.

Joseph opened the door wider and lit a lamp, illuminating the shadows of the interior. Mary had risen and picked up a sleeping Jesus. She sat on the stool with the child on her lap as the men alit from their beasts and entered the house. The servants remained with the animals.

Suddenly the house that had seemed so ample for their family now seemed very small. There was no conversation as one by one the elegant guests came forward, knelt before the now awakened child, pronounced a blessing in their native tongue and left. Three of them placed gifts in ornate bejeweled boxes on the floor in front of the child. Then they left as silently as they had come.

As Joseph shut the door, Mary looked in amazement at her son. He was wide awake and looked every bit a king who had just received tribute from his servants. Was this a dream, she wondered. No, the gifts were there on the floor – proof that it was real. Had God so publicized His Son that these wise men had traveled so very far to see Him? They had said that they had been traveling many months, following the star! Why had others not seen it? Did only those selected by God see this sign? Those who were seeking? She marveled at how God just kept reaffirming His Son.

Joseph knelt by the boxes and reverently opened each one. He saw in the first one, a silver box with an intricate design and sapphires, the resin frankincense. From his studies in the synagogue as a youth, he knew that this aromatic substance which was used in sacrificial offerings signified Jesus' status as priest. God's Son would be a priest, he reflected. In one of the Psalms prophesying the Messiah, King David said, "You are a priest forever according to the order of Melchizedek."

The second box, made of hammered gold and set with rubies, contained gold coins. This symbolized royalty. They were recognizing Jesus' status as king, Joseph thought, but what was his kingdom? Was it Israel or Heaven? Would He lead a mighty army and drive out the Romans, leading the nation as King David had done? This was the expectation of most of the Jews, but was that God's plan?

In the third box, which was made of bronze with emeralds set into the top and sides, Joseph found myrrh, an ingredient of anointing oil. This would symbolize Jesus' status as a healer. Was He going to heal his nation, Joseph mused. But, he remembered, myrhh was also used to embalm bodies. What did that mean? Death?

All of these gifts from distant lands were truly gifts for a king. And they had been presented to his son – God's Son – who they had called the King of the Jews! Joseph was struck again by the thought of the awesome responsibility he had assumed when he took Mary for his wife while she was bearing God's Son. God's Son!

When they returned to bed, Joseph fell into a fitful sleep. Suddenly there was a man in the room with him. He was the same man who had appeared to him in Kir Jarim. This time, Joseph was ready to hear what this messenger from God had to tell him.

"Arise," he said, "and take the young child and his mother. Flee to Egypt and stay there until I bring you word, for Herod will seek the child to destroy him."

Joseph was immediately awake. Although the angel was gone, he knew that he must obey without question, so he got up and went out to the donkey. He placed the packs on it and returned to the house where he began packing the items they would take with them. Mary and the baby were sleeping peacefully.

When the packs were full, he glanced at the unfinished table, but he knew that he would leave it and all the tools, for he could not take time to complete his work or have room to take the tools. Returning to the house, he gathered what food was already prepared and made a bundle which he would carry. He knelt down by Mary and gently aroused her.

"What is it?" she asked.

"I have received a vision from God that we must flee this very night to Egypt for Herod will seek to destroy our son," he answered. "Quickly get Him ready. I have loaded the donkey and have food in this bundle."

He stood up and looked around. There were the three boxes containing the gifts of the wise men. These must go, too, he thought as he picked up the first one and carried it out to the donkey. They were provided, he realized, to sustain us on our sojourn – however long it might be. Carefully he packed all three of the precious gifts – God had made His provision for them once again.

Joseph lifted Mary onto the back of the donkey and handed Jesus to her, then led the donkey out into the fields toward the road leading to Egypt.

When the wise men left the house of Joseph, they skirted the fields at the edge of the village. Leaving the town behind, they sought a good place to pitch their tents for the night. The light from the star aided the task and soon the camp was made. Silence prevailed for the few hours until dawn.

The smell of strong coffee made by the servants awoke the travelers and they came together to discuss their plans for the journey home, their mission accomplished.

"I could hardly believe that the Son of God would be found in such lowly circumstances," said one man, dressed in the flowing robes of the Persians.

"And yet," added the Indian, "that was definitely where the star led us."

"And it stayed right there," agreed the Arab.

"The father did not seem surprised by our appearance, did he?" asked the Chaldean.

"No," responded the Persian, "the only one who seemed surprised by us was King Herod."

"Yes, I would say that he was caught completely off guard."

"Why do you think he didn't know of the prophesies? They are found in the ancient writings and are very specific."

"You would think that he would know of such a significant event taking place in his own country."

"Do you really think that he wants to come and worship the child? I saw a flash of wickedness in his eye as he asked us to come and tell him where the child was"

"I saw it, too."

"I had a vision last night," said the Persian.

"What was it?" the others asked in chorus.

"A messenger told me that we should not return to Herod, but that we should return to our homes by a different route," he related.

"Then that is what we must do," stated the Indian and he called for his servant to bring the maps to him. As they were poring over the maps, one asked, "Should we warn the parents of the child?"

Immediately a messenger was dispatched to return to Joseph's house and warn them of the possibility of Herod's scheme. He returned by the time they had revised their routes and struck camp. He told them that the family had already gone – the house was deserted.

"Apparently, their God also sent His messenger to them during the night," surmised the Persian.

Missing

As usual, Rachel and Eli arose before the sun. By the time it crested the hill across the valley, Eli had gone to the field and Rachel was nursing Rueben. Jacob rubbed his eyes as he awoke and looked around. Everything seemed to be as it should be to his still drowsy mind, so he lay back down and closed his eyes again. When she finished with Rueben, Rachel began grinding the wheat. The sound aroused Jacob again and he got up.

When she finished with the grinding, Rachel prepared a small piece of lamb and some figs for Jacob to eat. As he ate, the little boy talked with his mother, telling her how much he loved Jesus and what they were going to do today. Rachel's mind was on laying the fire in her baking jar and she didn't really hear what he said. While the jar heated, she tended to Rueben's needs and kneaded the dough, which she patted out and placed on the jar. While the bread was baking, she made a second batch and then began to prepare the mid-morning meal for Eli.

Suddenly Rachel realized that Jacob wasn't in the room. Where had the boy gone? When she went to place Eli's meal on the table outside, she looked around for Jacob, but something was wrong. She guessed that he had gone across the street to see Jesus. Then she noticed that there were no sounds coming from Joseph's workshop.

She crossed the street and looked in Mary's door. There sat Jacob next to Jesus' cradle, but it was empty and Jacob was crying.

"Where is Jesus?" he sobbed. "I want to play with him."

Rachel went to him. He looked so pitiful. Big tears streamed down his face and his eyes had a completely baffled look. Rachel was mystified. What had happened? The bed had been used. Many of the household items were missing. Had they left? Where had they gone? Why hadn't they said anything? Last night Joseph said that he had promised a table and would finish it today.

She picked Jacob up and went to the shop at the back of the house. The unfinished table was still there, but the donkey was gone.

Did it have anything to do with the star? The night had been unusually bright on the first night they had met – the night that Jesus was born and they had commented on the brightness of the star that had appeared last night. Was there a connection? Every time she turned around it seemed that there were more questions, but no answers. She and Jacob were returning to their house when Eli came in for his meal.

"Eli, What do you think could have happened to our neighbors?" Rachel asked. "There is no one across the street. Even the donkey is gone, but the table Joseph mentioned is still there and still unfinished."

Jacob was sobbing. He was brokenhearted.

"I don't know. I'll go over and see," he answered. Eli returned as perplexed as his wife.

"What could have happened?" she asked.

"I wonder if Joseph said anything to Jonas. I'll go and see if he knows anything," Eli answered as he went out the door.

Jonas was as surprised as Eli and Rachel were. None of them could imagine what had happened. The family had just disappeared!

The questions were still unanswered two days later when Rachel went across the street again after Jacob. Jesus had drawn the boy the entire time He had been there and the magnetism was still there, even though the child wasn't. He had been Jacob's first friend.

"I know how much you miss Jesus," Rachel said as she knelt by the boy. "I miss his Mommy and Daddy, too, and so does Daddy, but they aren't here now, so you must come home and not come back over here unless they come back. You worry Mommy when you leave our house. Come on, now."

"No, I want to wait for Jesus here," cried Jacob as he planted his little feet firmly. Rachel picked Rueben up from Jesus' now unused cradle where she had placed him while she spoke with Jacob and, grasping the toddler's hand, started for the door.

Outside she heard the sounds of armor clanging and heard shrieks of terror and crying children. She felt a shudder of fear go down her spine. Something was terribly wrong. She tried to hurry across the street to the safety of her home, where she would bolt the door, but Jacob, not realizing anything but his own anguish pulled back. She gave him a yank to pull him off his defiant stance and took a few steps. Suddenly, she saw a soldier from Herod's guards running purposefully down the street toward her. Jacob saw the man, too, and began to cry with fear as he started to follow his mother, but it was too late.

The soldier raised his sword and swung it at the child, nearly cutting him in two. Then he grabbed Rachel's shoulder and swung her enough to flip Reuben from her arm. The baby had scarcely touched the dirt street when the soldier thrust his sword into him. The infant hadn't even let out a cry.

Spinning on his heel, the soldier turned and walked first to the door of her house and looked inside. Seeing nothing, he strode across the street and looked in Mary and Joseph's house. Satisfied that there was no one there, he ran down the street, nearly knocking over the stunned Eli, who had just come around the corner in time to see the slaughter.

The soldier's shove snapped Eli out of the stupor that had set in as he watched the murder of his sons. He now realized that Rachel was kneeling beside the tiny bodies. He rushed to her side. She wasn't even crying. She had gathered Reuben in her arms and pulled Jacob's head onto her lap and she was slowly rocking them as she did when she was lulling them to sleep. But there was no sound – no lullaby – only silence in the street and the sound of battle in the distance.

Eli took Jacob in his arms. Bitter tears fell on the boy's beautiful face as his father looked at him. With Eli's help, Rachel, still carrying Reuben, rose and walked into the house. Her face was stony, without color or expression. Her eyes were dry.

The Aftermath

Eli rose from the dusty street where he had been listlessly drawing figures that meant nothing. He could hear Deborah, his mother-in-law, still singing to his wife. I must try to tell her about Rachel, he thought. She will know what to do. Deborah looked up when he came in, but the lullaby didn't stop.

"Rachel has not once cried," Eli told Deborah. "In fact, she hasn't shown any emotion at all. I prepared our sons for burial and completed it by sunset that night. I have tried to talk to Rachel, but she doesn't respond. She just lays perfectly still on the sleeping mat and stares at the ceiling. Finally last night, I laid down beside her. She still didn't move. Several times during the night, I reached over to touch her, to make sure that she was still breathing. When I felt the shallow rise and fall of her chest, I cried myself back to sleep.

"What happened?" he cried. "Why did God take our precious sons – the gifts He had given us?" He heard the cries from all the other houses and knew that they were not the only ones who had suffered this loss, but the nagging question "Why?" was unanswerable.

"The next morning," Eli continued, "I awoke and rose. I didn't know what to do, but I needed to do something. I started a fire and heated some water for coffee, but Rachel refused to drink anything. I don't blame her! The coffee was terrible! When she finally moved, she scooted into the corner and pulled her feet up, sitting in a tight ball with her knees under her chin. Her eyes stared blankly at nothing. She stayed right there all day – never moving. She was completely inconsolable and unable to release her feelings. I managed to get her to lie down for the night, but the next morning, she again retreated to the corner, still refusing any help or care. And so you found her today," he concluded.

Deborah's lullaby seemed to help Rachel relax a bit from the terrible tenseness that had gripped her body since the awful event, but she refused to move from the corner. As evening approached, Deborah left her daughter and prepared some food for Eli and herself. She knew that neither of them had eaten anything before she arrived. She fixed Rachel's favorite meal, but again she refused to eat. Deborah knew that Eli was grateful for her efforts and for the food she prepared for him. She wanted to give him time to grieve, but she knew that she would probably be the one who would need to point a way out of this tragic event. She asked God for insight and direction before she went to sleep.

The next morning, Deborah arose and began doing regular household chores, singing a tune she had sung while working since Rachel was a child. Eli had gone to the field as soon as he had risen and would soon be returning for his mid-morning meal. She put some wheat in the grindstone and began turning it, still singing the tune. Rachel opened her eyes and looked at her. Deborah noted that her eyes were not glazed this morning.

"The bread will be ready soon," she said. Rachel got up and slowly walked to the door. She looked out toward the field. The new wheat had turned the field into a soft carpet of green. Birds were chirping and off in the distance, an ewe was bleating for its lamb. Rachel stood there until the bread was baked.

Deborah placed Eli's meal on the table by the door. She poured a cup of coffee and asked Rachel if she would like one, too. She was pleased when Rachel nodded. As she handed her daughter the cup, she whispered a prayer of thanksgiving to God.

Although Rachel got up and moved about, she did so as if she was in a trance. Most of the time, she just stood at the door and looked out. She didn't speak and she didn't make any attempt to fit into the household. She just was there. That evening, Deborah asked Eli to take a walk with her. She hated to have to say what she was going to, but felt that it was the only way to handle the situation.

"Eli," she began, "I fear that Rachel will never be able to come back from this event as long as she lives in this place, the scene of all her tragedy."

"I fear that you are right," Eli agreed. "What do you think we should do?"

"Perhaps, if she was living elsewhere, she would heal and return to normal again."

"Where would we go?" Eli asked. "I own this house and the land. I have never lived anywhere else. If we were to leave Bethlehem, I would need to sell my land and home so that we could begin again, but where?"

"True," Deborah responded, "but I feel that Rachel should leave very soon. See if this would work out for you. I will take her home with me so that the healing can begin. If you wanted to live in Bethany, you could sell your land and house and follow. You could stay with Daniel and me until you could get settled in your own home. By that time, we would hope and pray that Rachel would be healed enough to be able to function. I don't know if she would ever be able to come back here to live. The memories might make it unbearable."

They stopped and Eli looked out over his fields, now bathed in moonlight. These fields had provided them with a good living. If he were to leave, he would be leaving behind the two sons he had so loved, too. Could he cut all these ties?

Deborah broke the silence.

"I know that this is a big decision, Eli. You must pray about it and come to the answer that you can live with. Either way, Rachel and I will leave right away. If you decide to stay in Bethlehem, she can return if she heals from this condition. I know that this is a terrible decision, but when you know what you want to do, you will tell us." With that, she returned to the house, leaving Eli to ponder the problem.

These fields meant a great deal to Eli. They were the means by which he had provided for his family – the family that no longer existed. They had been a mark of great achievement for him. He had not inherited them, but by the diligence of his labor, and the favor of a loving God working through a kindly, childless man, he had acquired them. Now he must take stock and see what path to take from this point.

He fell to the ground and lay prostrate. Praying to God for guidance and direction, his tears watered the fertile soil. He prayed for a long time, then just lay there waiting for God's answer.

When the sun rose in the morning, Deborah was making preparations to take Rachel home with her. If Eli had made a decision, he hadn't told her yet. He had stayed out in the field all night. Shortly before dawn, he returned and immediately left the house, not waking anyone to say where he was going. Deborah gathered Rachel's clothes and prepared a mid-morning meal for Eli, baking up what bread she could make from the wheat that was on hand. Then she prepared a meal to take to be eaten on their trip to Bethany. She was sweeping the floor when Eli returned.

"Mother," he began, "I went to see a man I know who once told me that he had a relative who wanted to take up farming here. He is going to talk with the relative and we'll see what kind of arrangement we can make. If we can find agreement, I'll be moving to Bethany soon. Then we can help Rachel together." Deborah smiled and whispered a prayer of thanksgiving.

Deborah and Rachel left soon after Eli returned. He pressed into Deborah's hand a small bag containing the money Rachel had gathered with her bread enterprise during the census.

"It can be used as necessary to care for her," he said.

It was still early when they left the house so they could be in Bethany before dusk. In order to brighten Rachel's mood, Deborah talked with her about events in her childhood. She had been such a cheerful child, always singing. If she wasn't singing, Deborah knew that she was either in trouble or going to jump out and surprise her. That had become one of Rachel's favorite games very early in her life. She had missed those "attacks" when marriage had taken her daughter so far away.

The trip was going well. They crossed the valley and passed the ridge so that Bethlehem was no longer in sight when they stopped for their mid-morning meal. As they sat on stones near the road and ate bread, nuts and dates, Rachel remembered the little outing she and Mary had with the children only a few weeks earlier. The pent-up grief burst through her defenses. Suddenly she began sobbing. Deborah held her closely, rocked her and smoothed her hair as she had done so many years ago to soothe her.

Passersby looked at the pair and walked on. This was not an uncommon sight these days. Some had been through the same ordeal and understood. When the wracking sobs lessened and Rachel regained her composure, they picked up the bundles of belongings and continued their journey into a new life.

Eli came a week later. The man he had spoken with had told his relative that Eli's fields were the finest in the Bethlehem area. He came to see them and immediately struck a bargain whereby he would rent the fields and the house for a year. If at the end of that time, he was satisfied, he would purchase them.

It took Eli only a day to buy a donkey and cart, load it with all they had and reach Bethany. What he found there heartened him greatly. Rachel seemed almost like her old self. True, she was slightly more subdued and she didn't sing, but she did smile at him when he came through the door and when they went to bed that night, she lay very close to him. The two became inseparable from that time on.

Daniel offered to teach Eli the potter's trade and bring him into the business with himself and Samuel. Knowing that this would keep him near Rachel most of the time, he agreed. Daniel was impressed at how earnest his new student was. Although his hands were large, the field work had strengthened them so that it was easy for him to work the clay. It was not long before he was turning out credible bowls, with very few rejects.

In the second week of their stay with Rachel's family, Daniel drew Eli aside and suggested that if he wanted to build a house on the land adjacent to his house, he and Samuel would help him. Eli gladly accepted the offer and in the following week, the project began. The three men worked at the pottery in the morning and in the late afternoon and early evening of the long summer days built a house for Rachel.

Eli wanted to give her the house she had yearned for in Bethlehem, so Daniel and Samuel helped him build a two room dwelling with a usable roof where she could lay out the clothes to dry or prepare dates and figs for storage with a small room where a guest could stay if they had visitors. It also had an extended roof where she could sit on hot afternoons and do some of her chores in the cool breezes that made the summer days more tolerable. They even built an outdoor oven in which she could bake loaves of bread. That would mean that Eli wouldn't have fresh-baked bread twice a day as when she had baked on the jars, but it would make life easier for his wife and that made him happy – a small sacrifice to make for so great a reward.

Upon completion of the house, they moved their belongings in and Rachel busied herself with setting up housekeeping. Deborah didn't help her. She knew that this was part of the healing process, although she often peeked in with a cheery word of encouragement. Only once did she see Rachel overcome with grief.

PART II

Interlude

The days passed and turned into months. Then one bright spring day, Rachel came to Deborah's door. Her face was aglow. It was a different Rachel who told her that she was expecting a baby. Deborah flew to her and embraced her. She was well again.

The baby girl was born that fall. They named her Naomi, because as Rachel said, "She is 'My Delight'." She was a pleasant child and didn't make a fuss, but giggled and cooed her delight with her world.

Naomi was just learning to walk when Rachel's second baby was born. "Pure and bright" seemed to be the perfect description of her, so they called her Phoebe. She wanted attention and Naomi was glad to give it to her. They entertained each other so well that Rachel didn't worry about them at all. Even when they began to walk, they were content to stay in the house where they watched their mother and imitated her tasks. Rachel had begun to hum again while she worked. And she smiled often as she watched her daughters at play.

It was three years before baby Jesse arrived. Deborah had suggested the name, because Rachel had finally come to realize that "God exists." Jesse gave Eli a special gift. While they loved and were thankful for their daughters, this son would continue the line, especially important to a man. No man wanted his name to be lost.

Eli was quite adept now at the potter's trade and when Daniel died, he and Samuel continued operating the business together. Eli found that he also had a gift for selling their wares. They were now taking two carts full to market and coming home empty. The family was flourishing in every way. Samuel still lived with Deborah, but now he had a bride, Sarah. The two women worked well together and grew to love each other. It was with great joy that they tended to Sarah and Samuel's new baby, Caleb. He was a robust child and kept everyone busy.

As Rachel's girls grew, they assumed more and more of the housekeeping responsibilities. Naomi particularly loved to bake and eagerly took to that daily task. Phoebe liked to work in the soil and soon had a garden full of good things to eat – lentils, beans, cucumbers, onions, beets and potatoes. She had even planted some grape seeds and started vines. She sought instruction from a neighbor and soon had a small vineyard. Eli built an arbor for the vines to grow on and many a summer day, both of the girls would be found under the arbor shelling beans or preparing grapes for drying into raisins.

The girls would take turns going to the well for water. That was a place to socialize with other girls of the village. Both disliked working at the loom, but they both liked clothes, so they did their share of the weaving and sewing. Before Rachel was ready for it, both of her daughters had grown up and were of the age to get married.

Naomi's Story

Simon, Naomi's betrothed, was a young man she had met on one of the rare trips she made with her father to Jerusalem on market day. She loved the excitement of the milling crowd. The savory smells of the bakery and fruit stalls – the pungent aromas of spices from distant countries and just the people themselves all mingled together. She marveled at the sight of all the wares that filled the stalls – clothes, jewelry, rugs, perfumes – things she had never seen before. Things that were bought by the wealthy who lived in Jerusalem – priests and members of the king's court and wealthy merchants. She didn't go far, as she had a healthy fear of getting lost, but one day she was looking back into one of the stalls as she started walking and ran right into a young man who was talking to the merchant in the next booth, hitting him so hard that she knocked him down.

"Oh, I'm terribly sorry," she stammered as she noticed the fine clothes he was wearing. "I should have been looking where I was going."

"I'm not hurt at all," he assured her, but he remained seated on the street.

"Then why aren't you getting up?" she asked. The impact had knocked her head scarf loose and she self-consciously fumbled with it, trying to capture the strands of hair that had escaped. She offered her hand to help him rise and he looked into her eyes.

"Because I like the view," he answered. "If I get up, you'll hurry away and I won't even know your name. What is your name?" He saw that she was just a country girl, but her manner was captivating and her eyes were so sincere. She intrigued him.

"My name is Naomi," she told him as she placed her hand nearer to him. "Now, please get up. Everyone is staring and you might get walked on or run over by one of the push carts."

He reached for her hand, but he continued to hold on to it when he was on his feet. She tried to pull away, but he took her other hand in his other hand and they stood face to face.

"My name is Simon. I live in Jerusalem," he stated. "Where do you live?"

"I live in Bethany," she answered as she again tried to pull her hands from his, but his grasp did not release.

"And what are you doing in Jerusalem alone?"

"I'm not alone. I am with my father and uncle."

"Where are they? I don't see them."

"They are at the pottery stall in the marketplace."

"You shouldn't be wandering about alone. Come, I'll escort you back to them," he said, still holding one of her hands. They headed down the street toward the marketplace. When they reached the pottery stall, Eli looked from his daughter to Simon and back again. Simon finally released Naomi's hand.

"We had missed you," Eli said to her.

"I found your daughter, or rather, she found me," Simon laughed. "I did not want her to be wandering about the streets alone, so I brought her back to you safely."

"I am grateful," Eli responded.

"Are you here every market day," Simon asked.

"Yes, I am," answered Eli, "but my daughter is not."

Simon laughed again, tipped his hat to Eli and Naomi, turned and strode down the street.

As Naomi approached the village well, she was startled to see the young man from the marketplace last week sitting on the adjacent wall. She also saw several of the girls who were getting water looking flirtatiously at him. I wonder what he is doing here, she thought as she set her jar down and took the rope from around her waist. She tied it to the handle of the jar so that she could lower it.

Suddenly he was at her elbow.

"May I help you with that?" he asked.

"No," she answered. "I have it tied."

"Then let me lower it for you" he insisted. His voice sounded authoritative and polished. She allowed him to take the rope. He lowered the jar, then raised the filled jar and placed it on the wall. He untied the rope and Naomi again secured it around her waist, picked up the jar and set it on her head. She began to walk away and Simon walked beside her. She glanced nervously at him, not turning her head. Simon saw it and smiled to himself.

"Where are you going?" she asked.

"Wherever you are going," he answered.

"You can't," she told him.

"Why not?"

"It isn't proper."

"I need to know where you live so that I can speak with your father."

"What do you need to say?"

"It is man talk."

"Well, you will find him in the pottery shop. Good day," she said, gesturing toward the shop as she turned toward her house.

Simon entered the shop and saw Eli, who was sitting at the potter's wheel. A glance from Eli told Simon that he had been noticed. Another man was just walking out the doorway at the back of the shop when he entered, so he sat down on a ledge near the door. When the wheel stopped, the exquisite bowl on it was finished. The graceful lines made it stand out among the ordinary bowls already lining the shelf on the opposite wall.

"A special order," explained Eli.

"It is worthy of a great purpose. Who is it to go to?" asked Simon.

"This bowl is to be used in the Temple," stated Eli.

"You are a master at your trade," observed Simon.

"You did not come here to watch me work," Eli broke in. "Aren't you the young man who brought my daughter back at the market last week? What is your name and what is your purpose?"

Simon laughed. "You are most perceptive, too. I did come for another purpose. My name is Simon, son of Benjamin the spice merchant."

Eli waited. Simon lost his self-assured demeanor. Looking down at the floor, he began, "I came to see if your daughter, Naomi, was spoken for in marriage. I know that you probably weren't expecting this, especially as I have not been with her other than the few minutes in the market. Still, I knew at once that she was to be my wife."

Eli was stunned. Before him stood a young man who was obviously wealthy from the clothing he wore and his genteel manner. And he was asking for Naomi to be his wife. Was he really serious, Eli wondered.

"You're right," he answered, "why would you be interested in my Naomi? We are not wealthy as you are."

"I'm not even sure what it was," Simon answered. "All I know is that I cannot even think about anything else since I met her."

"What does your father say about this? Does he even know you are here with this question?" Eli asked.

"He knows," Simon replied. "When he saw that I was in such a state, he told me to come here and get done whatever I had to in order to regain my senses. So I came and sat down by the well, watching the girls come for water. When I saw Naomi, I could hardly contain myself. My heart longed to have her with me for the rest of my life, so I walked her home and came to see you."

"Does your father know that the object of your ardor is the daughter of a tradesman, not a noble?" Eli queried.

"We have had a serious talk about it and he has agreed that if I truly want her for my wife, it should be put to you. If you agree, we will dispatch our deputy to meet yours whenever you say. My father also married a tradesman's daughter and she has been the light of his life. I believe with my whole heart that Naomi is the light of my life."

"Does Naomi know that you are asking for her?"

"We have not spoken of this matter."

I must discuss your request with my wife and daughter, Eli thought. "I will let you know in two days when I return to the marketplace," he told the young man. "You can come that day and I will give you my answer."

"Agreed," said Simon and he turned and left. His step had a lightness in it.

When Eli came home for the evening meal, he told Rachel that he needed to talk with her and Naomi. Rachel had seen the young man walking by Naomi when she returned from the well go to the potter's shop. When she had asked Naomi what he wanted of her father, the reply had been "I don't know." Rachel suspected his purpose, even if Naomi didn't, and this conference Eli called seemed to confirm her suspicions. She told Phoebe and Jesse to clean things up and went outside to join Eli and Naomi.

As she came and sat down beside Eli, she remarked, "I saw that you had a visitor today."

"Yes," he confirmed, looking at Naomi sitting opposite him. "The young man is named Simon bar Benjamin the spice merchant. That is a very wealthy family and one of the most revered in Jerusalem." Naomi's heart leaped as she now began to suspect what he had come for.

"He met Naomi when she was in Jerusalem with me last week," continued Eli. "He walked her back to the stall after she went exploring. He was very polite and correct in his ways. Today he told me he had come to the well to see our Naomi. He had told his father that he wanted to take Naomi for his wife and he said that his father agreed to whatever decision he made. He came here today to see if his heart still wanted her, and it did. So he came to see me. I told him that I needed to consider the matter and would give him an answer on market day next."

"Have you made a decision?" asked Rachel.

"Not yet. How do you feel about this?" he asked his wife.

"I know that Naomi is nearly the age to marry, but I thought that she would marry someone from Bethany," Rachel responded. " I don't know if I want her to leave this town. I know that Jerusalem is not that far and we could see her often, but it would almost be like losing her. And we don't know her people either."

"Do you have anything to say, Naomi?" asked her father.

"I am surprised by this thing," she answered. "I was pleased when he showed me attention. He looked so fine, but I didn't think he saw me as anything but a foolish girl."

"What did you think when you saw him at the well this morning?"

"I was surprised and bewildered. I couldn't see why he would come to Bethany. I doubt that he had ever been here before. Then he asked to see you and I thought that he wanted to buy a piece of pottery and didn't want to wait until market day."

"Would you be content to be his wife?" asked her mother.

"I think I would be if he was kind to me," she answered.

"There is no doubt that he would give a fine dowry," Rachel said.

"True," Eli agreed. "But is that the most important consideration?"

"Am I then to be betrothed to Simon?" Naomi asked.

"I do not know yet," he answered, "we will pray on the matter until we get an answer." With that he led the family in their first prayer on Naomi's betrothal. It was now in God's hands and they knew that God would hear their prayers and would guide them to the right decision.

The next day, when Eli and Samuel were working at their wheels, Eli broached the subject.

"You saw the young man who came to the shop yesterday?"

"Yes, but he was gone by the time I returned from the kiln. Did he buy something?"

"No, but he asked for something – Naomi's hand in marriage."

Samuel gasped. "Isn't he the young man we met so briefly on market day last?"

"The very same."

"Was he serious?"

"Very serious."

"What do you know about him?"

"Very little, really, but he is the son of the spice merchant in Jerusalem – you know, the one who does all the business with the Temple."

"Why would the son of such a wealthy family be at all interested in Naomi? She is a beautiful young woman and very engaging, but …"

"I know, but he was very sincere in his request. If he is truly desirous of making her his wife, do you think it would be a good marriage?"

"I suppose it could be, if he is as sincere as you think him to be."

"Samuel, you are a man I would trust with the most precious part of my life. Let's explore this thing further and see if his intentions are as honorable as they seem. I told him that I would give him my answer on market day. Would you be my arbitrator and meet with their representative to negotiate Naomi's betrothal?"

"I am honored that you would trust me with such a responsibility. Thank you."

"After the meal tonight, we will meet to discuss details."

On the next market day, Samuel went to the spice store owned by Simon's father.

"I have come," he began, "to speak with Benjamin regarding his son, Simon."

The servant nodded and went to find Benjamin. Samuel knew immediately that the self-assured, well-dressed merchant approaching him was Benjamin.

"I understand that you are here about my son, Simon," he said with a smile.

"Yes," Samuel answered, "Eli the Potter, father of Naomi, has authorized me to act as his representative in the matter to be addressed today regarding his daughter's possible betrothal to your son, Simon."

"Ah, yes," Benjamin smiled again. "He was so smitten with the girl that he couldn't keep his wits about him, so I told him to go and get it settled. When he returned from a visit to your village, he said that he was hopeful and that he would receive an answer from her father today. Do you have an answer?"

"The answer is yes if the brideprice is right."

"Ah, yes," Benjamin again said. "What would the girl's father expect as a fair price?"

"For the hand of Naomi," Samuel began, "her parents would expect at least four sets of fine clothing, a fatted calf and a goodly amount of spices. They would have a house built near Bethany so the couple could live near to them. And Naomi should have a servant when she goes to her husband's home."

"But what else do her parents want for themselves," pressed Benjamin.

"They will be satisfied with the items I have listed," responded Samuel. "Their daughter's future is the most important thing they want. If Simon is kind and gentle to her and a good father to their children; if they will live near enough for frequent visits, these are the things that mean the most to them."

Benjamin smiled. "The parents of Naomi are good to their daughter and I would like for my son to have such fine in-laws. Surely, a daughter raised in such a home would be a fine wife. The terms are reasonable and I agree. The betrothal will be celebrated one month from today."

The agreement was sealed and one month later, Naomi and Simon were betrothed in a joyous two-day celebration. Their betrothal, according to custom, was an arrangement like marriage, but the final consummation would wait until the wedding was celebrated in about a year. In the meantime, Naomi would spend a great deal of time with Simon's mother and learn how to maintain a refined household. She would learn what things pleased her husband and all of the duties she would be expected to perform. She would find that there would be servants to perform many of the mundane tasks her mother did, but there were other requirements made of her.

They moved into the fine home Simon had built for her on a hilltop at the edge of the village on the day of their wedding and Naomi was delighted to find that from their upstairs bedroom she could see her parents' home and the pottery shop.

The house seemed quieter now that the wedding was over and Naomi was no longer living with them, Rachel thought as she kneaded the bread. She had gone to live with her new husband in the beautiful big home he had built for her. She was adapting well to her new life and was making a place for herself in the life of the village.

Rachel, too, had accepted that she only had two children at home to care for and watch over. It wasn't that there was less work to do, because Naomi had spent so much of the time the past year in Jerusalem with Simon's family that she had already adjusted to that part. It was that she was feeling that her fledglings were leaving the nest. Yes, that was what they were supposed to do, but protecting them and nurturing them in every way since their births had been her sole focus in life. She had been so afraid that something terrible might happen to one or all of them and she would lose them, too, just as Jacob and Reuben had been lost. Rachel knew that she could not have prevented those deaths, but she still mourned them and vowed that she would not let these children down. Now they would leave one by one and her reason for living would be gone again. She feared what would become of her when they were all in their own homes and not depending on her any longer.

She shook her head as she carefully formed the loaves and placed them on the board to take to the oven. No, she would not allow such thoughts to strip her of the blessings she still had. She would have the satisfaction of knowing that she and Eli had raised strong children and they would have each other when the children had found their own lives.

The Miracle

Phoebe entered the room and quickly set the filled water jar in its accustomed place. She saw her mother at the loom.

"Mother," she began excitedly, "you know what I heard at the well this morning? 'It's impossible,' I told them, but they insisted that it was true. Can you believe it?"

"I don't know unless you tell me what was said," her mother responded.

"Sarah and Abigail were saying that Lazarus, the man who has the olive trees, had died and the man who people say is a prophet made him alive again," she answered.

"Slow down and start at the beginning."

"They said that Lazarus' two sisters had sent for the prophet," Phoebe began again, but Rachel interrupted. "You mean the man they call Jesus?"

"Yes, that one," she continued. "Lazarus had been sick a few days and his sisters were sure that he would die, so they sent word to Jesus and asked him to come right away."

"Did he come?" Rachel asked.

"Not right away. He came about a week later and by that time Lazarus had been dead four days."

"I know. I heard the mourners at their house."

"Well, that's when Jesus showed up. They took him to the tomb and he told those with them to roll back the stone. Everyone expected the awful stink, but Jesus called for Lazarus to come out of the tomb. And he did!"

"He came out? Was he really dead? Are they sure that he was dead?"

"One of his sisters accused Jesus of delaying too long. She said that if He had come right away, her brother would not have died."

"This is hard to believe," Rachel said, "I will go to see Mary. Phoebe, will you start laying out the things for your father and Jesse's evening meal?" Leaving things in her daughter's hands, Rachel hurried out the door.

Others were at the home when Rachel approached and Mary and Martha were answering their questions. According to what she heard, everything Phoebe had said was confirmed. It had truly been a miracle! Satisfied, Rachel returned home and related the exciting news to Eli, who had just come into the house from the pottery shop. All during the evening, the family mulled over the miraculous story and wondered about its significance.

During the night, Rachel began to wonder about something, so the next morning after she finished her usual work, she went again to the house of Lazarus. Mary was just returning from the well with her jar of water and Rachel walked beside her.

"Phoebe told me that your brother is alive," Rachel began.

"Yes," Mary answered, "we still can hardly believe it, but it's true."

"He was really dead?" Rachel pressed.

"He had been so sick and Martha sent for Jesus to come and heal him," Mary explained, "but he didn't come for nearly a week and by then, it was too late for healing."

"I heard the mourners this week," Rachel said.

"Lazarus died six days ago and we buried him in the tomb. Then the mourners came and many important people even came from Jerusalem."

"He has been well known and respected by many of the leaders," Rachel agreed.

"Yes, and the house was full of them, both merchants and priests, the day that Jesus arrived," Mary continued. "Martha saw Him coming up the road and went out to meet Him. She told Him that Lazarus had died and was buried. He wept for Lazarus and then He wanted to go to the tomb, so Martha sent for me to join them. Everyone else came with me. Let me put this jar down and we can walk out to the olive garden." Mary went into the house and returned in a minute to continue their walk.

"What happened at the tomb?" asked Rachel.

"Everyone was standing there and Jesus told them to roll back the stone which sealed it. Martha protested. After all, he had been in there four days and would be stinking by that time, but Jesus insisted, so some of the men moved the stone. There was no smell! We were amazed! And then Jesus called, 'Lazarus, come out' and he did! In a minute he was standing in the doorway, still wrapped in the grave clothes."

"Standing? He had risen and was standing? Could it be true?" gasped Rachel.

"Yes, it is true! He walked to the house and dressed and ate and drank with the visitors from Jerusalem. It was unbelievable, but true."

"Your family is visited frequently by Jesus. He is a close friend?" she asked.

"Yes," Mary answered. "He is always a welcome visitor."

"Do you know the rest of His family."

"Not really. Why do you ask?"

"I was wondering if I might have met Him somewhere before. Or if maybe I knew his mother. What is her name?" Rachel asked excitedly.

"Her name is Mary."

"And his father?" Rachel pressed.

"His name is Joseph, but he died a few years ago."

"What was his livelihood?"

"He was a carpenter. He taught Jesus to be a carpenter, but he turned to preaching as soon as his brothers were old enough to provide for the family."

"Where does His family live?" Mary urged.

"They live in Nazareth. Why are you so curious about them?" Mary asked.

"I have been wondering if I had known His parents when He was just a baby. He is about the age their baby would be now. The names seem to fit, but the place is wrong. The couple I knew were in Bethlehem." Suddenly a thought came to Rachel and she added "but they had come from Nazareth for the census. The baby was born while they were there and they decided to stay a while. Do you suppose that baby is this Jesus?"

"I guess that he could be," Mary responded.

"His birth was announced to some shepherds as that of the Son of God, but he seemed like any other baby to us," Rachel continued. "We became good friends, but suddenly one night the family vanished. We never knew what happened to them."

"That must have been right before you returned to Bethany," commented Mary.

"Yes," agreed Rachel, "it was two days later that Herod's soldiers came and killed my sons and my mother brought me back home with her. I often wondered what had happened to them. We never knew."

"I pray that someday you will know the answer to your questions," Mary replied as the two women parted to return to their homes.

Phoebe's Story

Jesse could be such a pest, Phoebe thought, as she picked up the shuttle she had dropped when he startled her. Her little brother should have been helping their father with the chores at the pottery shop instead of trying to scare her. He was still such a child. She, on the other hand, was becoming quite grown up. As she restarted the shuttle across the loom, she realized that she no longer minded weaving. It was a good time to let her mind dwell on other things. As the shuttle click clacked back and forth, she found herself musing about the boys in town.

There is Eleazer, her best friend Joanna's brother, she thought. He was kind and gentle and would probably be a good provider as he was a farmer, but he was so shy that he rarely spoke to her, even when she was with Joanna.

Then there is Jonathan, Abigail's brother. He was big and strong and would probably be a blacksmith like their father. A blacksmith always held a good position in a village as his was such a specialized trade. Phoebe smiled. He was always laughing and having a good time with life. That's why he had so many friends.

Adam is the oldest of a large family of boys. His father is the rabbi and he will probably be a rabbi, too. Phoebe didn't know if she wanted to be a rabbi's wife, but that probably didn't matter, because she didn't think Adam even knew she existed.

Aaron has been a close friend since she was very small. They had been playmates often because their mothers were friends. Together, Aaron and Phoebe had made Naomi's life miserable for a while, until their mothers put an end to it. She saw Aaron often at the well as they both had the task of drawing water for their families, and they still joked around with each other, but she had seen a closeness developing between him and Anna, so she guessed that he would just be a friend.

There were other boys in the village who may have thought about her, but they had kept their thoughts to themselves. Phoebe wondered if she would ever be spoken for and married as her sister now was.

Naomi was always the prettiest, but Phoebe knew that she would make a better wife. If only someone else saw that in her.

The evening meal was finished and the family was sitting outside their door talking about the events of the day, when the old man came up. He spoke for a moment with Eli and the two men strolled out toward the hills, deep in conversation. Phoebe recognized the old man as Eleazer's grandfather. He had been a farmer, but he had gradually given the farming chores over to his son and his family as he grew older. She wondered what they were talking about and soon her curiosity got the best of her. She excused herself and walked down the street a few doors before she ducked between two houses and made her way to a concealed spot near where her father and the man were talking.

Just then, the men shook hands and Eli said, "I'll have Samuel speak with you on the matter in a day or two." Then they parted, each to his own home. Phoebe wondered. Samuel had negotiated Naomi's betrothal. Could it be that her father was sending him on the same mission for her? She hurried back the way she had come and when she entered the house, her father wasn't there.

In a few minutes, Eli and Samuel came into the house and asked Rachel and Phoebe to join them. Jesse, too, was allowed to be a part of the group.

"What did Baruch want?" asked Rachel.

"Phanuel asked his father to represent him and his son in negotiations for the betrothal of our Phoebe," Eli answered as he looked at Phoebe, who wore a look of complete surprise.

"Eleazer wants me to be his wife?" she gasped.

"Yes, and I have asked Samuel to represent us," replied her father. Samuel nodded his acceptance of the role.

"Now the questions are – would this be a good match for you, Phoebe, and if so, what should we expect as dowry?" he said, watching his daughter's response.

Phoebe blushed. She had not expected Eleazer to be even thinking of such a thing. He hadn't even seemed to notice her when she was with Joanna and now he was proposing such a permanent arrangement. Her father smiled.

"I can see that you were not expecting this," he said. "Do you need some time to think about it?"

"Yes," she answered as she stood and walked out the door. Jesse followed her.

"Don't you want to marry Eleazer?" he asked when they were outside.

"I don't know," she answered, "I hardly know him."

"But you've known him all of your life."

"I've known Joanna all of my life and I know that he's her brother, but I don't know him at all. He has hardly ever spoken to me in all of these years. I don't know anything about who he is really. How can I think about spending the rest of my life with him? I don't know if he's gentle or cruel."

"You've never seen him hurt anything, have you," interrupted Jesse.

"No," she answered.

"You know that he is always working with his father in the fields, don't you?"

"Yes, but how would he be to me?"

"I don't know Eleazer very well, either, but I think he would be a fine husband for you," offered Jesse.

"Why do you think that?" challenged Phoebe.

"I know that his father thinks he is a hard worker and is becoming a good farmer, so he will be able to provide well for you. When he was going to synagogue for studies, he was well-thought of by his teachers. From what I have seen of him, everything he does, he puts his whole heart into and does it well, so I think he would be a good husband, too. I think that he would want you to be happy and content in your life with him, don't you?"

"Maybe, but the point is that I still don't know him. Still, when I was thinking about the boys in the village the other day, he came first to my mind." They walked on a little farther in silence before turning for home. By the time they entered the door, Phoebe had decided to accept whatever decision her father and Samuel made.

The next day Samuel met with Baruch and the betrothal was arranged. Eleazer's family would give Phoebe's family ten female goats and a ram. The betrothal would take place one month after Passover next week, so the preparations began immediately.

Passover

The predawn was alive with excitement. Deborah's family was going to celebrate Passover in Jerusalem. It had been several years since they had been able to go as a family. Usually, someone had stayed in Bethany to host other family members who had journeyed for Passover, but were unable to stay in Jerusalem. Now all of Deborah's children and their families, forty-six people in all, would make the joyous journey together. The midmorning meal would be shared before they reached the city gate. It would be a good time for family fellowship and visiting with each other and for the children to enjoy their cousins. It was a time of glorious confusion. Once in the city, they would go separate ways and stay with different families until the final day when they would meet again outside the city gate and return home together.

The men packed the six animals they would take with them to carry all the food and personal belongings they would need to have for the three-day-long celebration. The women finished their packing and brought food and bundles of clothing for the men to load on the animals. Children, filled with the exuberance of youth and excitement, ran here and there and everywhere. They would have the responsibility of herding the sacrificial animals the family would need for the celebration. Not only must they get them to Jerusalem, but the animals must get there unblemished.

By the time the sun was well up in the sky, everything was ready and the troop set off. Soon they joined the other family groups headed to the Holy City. The celebration had already begun. Someone began to sing and soon the whole throng was singing songs of praise as they walked.

A little before they reached the descent into the Kidron Valley, Deborah stated that they should stop for their midmorning meal. The men led the animals into a roadside field and the rest followed. Blankets were spread on the ground. The men unloaded the food from the animals and the older children took the bundles to their mothers who distributed it. Laughter filled the air. When members of the party were rejuvenated, the animals were reloaded and the group resumed their journey, singing as they walked down the Mount of Olives and across the Kidron Valley, up the ascent and through the city gate.

Simon's parents, Benjamin and Miriam, had invited Rachel, Eli, Phoebe and Jesse together with Naomi and Simon to stay at their house. Rachel was pleased to see how near it was to Temple Mount. This would be the first time that they had been so near the nearly completed edifice.

When Rachel saw the house of Simon's parents, she gasped. The massive walls were decorated with frescos of scenes of far-off countries where spices originate. In the center of the wall facing the Temple were elaborately carved double doors that were far taller than even a person on horseback.

Simon gave the lion's head knocker a rap and a moment later one of the massive doors swung open. Simon and Naomi stepped forward and beckoned the rest of the family to follow them. They entered the courtyard of the magnificent residence, and were shown to nearby benches. Two servants came with basins and towels and washed the dust from their feet. This gave Rachel a chance to take in the beauty of the home of Naomi's father and mother-in-law.

On three sides of the courtyard were pillared porches. Draperies were at each of the doorways off these porches, some of which were draped to one side and tied back revealing the room beyond. At either corner of the back section were stairways to the second story, which also had porches on the three sides. The windows on the rooms were covered by elaborate lattices and the whole building was whitewashed. The house had a roof of baked clay tiles which glistened in the sunlight and at the corners were long pipes leading from the roof to the cisterns under the courtyard. By collecting the rain from the roof, the house was assured of an ample water supply.

Near the entrance door on one side was the place which Rachel recognized as the area in which food was prepared. There were two ovens and a large storeroom with a table and many jars. On the other side of the entrance was a small pen sheltered by a thatch roof in which were several animals. Eli unloaded the donkey and put it and the two lambs they had brought in the pen with the other animals. The other lambs had accompanied the families who brought them to the quarters they were occupying during the celebration.

There were many rooms on the ground floor of the house. The party was ushered into the large one in the center. The floors immediately caught Rachel's eyes. They were beautiful with intricate mosaic designs. The walls of the room were finished to look like marble. It was so elegant!

Benjamin and Miriam were seated in chairs trimmed with ivory and seats padded with crimson fabric. They stood and greeted each of their guests. When they were all seated, the conversations began. Someone listening would have thought that they had known each other a lifetime.

"It looks like the city will be full for Passover this year," observed Eli.

"The streets are so full already that they don't seem to be able to hold any more," Benjamin agreed.

"I would think that the crowds would mean an increase in your business," Eli ventured.

"Not from the crowds, but from the Temple I have a great increase. The more sacrifices that are offered, the greater the need for my spices."

"True. How are your other children?"

"Ephriam, my oldest son, and his wife are not coming to Passover this year," Benjamin responded and the two men continued their conversation. Eli really enjoyed talking with Benjamin and Rachel and Miriam had discovered that they had much in common.

"I have been admiring the beautiful floors. How they brighten the room!" Rachel exclaimed. This was the first time that she and Eli had been to the spice merchant's house as the wedding had taken place at Simon and Naomi's newly built home in Bethany.

"Yes, I love them. It is quite a change from the dirt floors in the house of my father. He was a seller of fine clothing. What else could he be with a family of nine daughters and one son?" Miriam laughed. "Mother taught us to weave garments with intricate patterns as soon as we were old enough and with ten looms going six days a week, he had a good stock to take to market."

"Who bought the clothes? I make all that my family needs and I don't even know anyone who buys clothes, especially adorned ones," Rachel responded.

"He brought them to the market here in Jerusalem and the wealthy bought them. That's how I met Benjamin. He was passing by the stall one day when I accompanied Father. He usually took one of the daughters to show people how lovely the garments looked when they were worn."

Simon and Naomi saw that Phoebe and Jesse were not interested in the conversations of the elders, so they took them to see the city.

The young people returned shortly before the evening meal was ready. They had met some of Simon's friends and enjoyed the afternoon.

When the conversations slowed a bit, Miriam took Eli and Rachel to a lovely room on the second floor that had windows facing the street. The latticework concealed Rachel, but allowed her to look out. She stood for a long time at the window and watched the people passing in the street below. It was such a different perspective and she enjoyed the sense of observing them without their knowing.

Shopkeepers would soon be closing up their shops and hurrying home to begin observance of the holy celebration which began at sundown. As she watched the hustling crowd, she saw him – The Prophet, Jesus – and his followers coming down the street. Then she saw the woman following a little behind him. She recognized Mary, her long-ago friend.

I must speak with her, Rachel thought. I can catch up with her. She ran down the stairs, past Eli, who was in the courtyard talking to Simon, and out the outer door. She turned the corner, but the group she was trying to catch up to was nowhere to be seen. Where could they have gone?

She walked on a little way, but the crowd pushed and jostled her, slowing her down. Still she did not see the group she was looking for. They had been heading away from the Temple, so she turned that direction.

She turned down another street filled with people, but she didn't see them there either. Another turn. Still no one. Suddenly Rachel was aware that she was on a much quieter street. There were no people on it at all. And she didn't know where she was. How foolish she was to have gone out by herself in a city where she was a stranger!

She neared a door where she heard voices. Perhaps someone there would help her get back to Benjamin's house. She walked toward the door, but what she heard alarmed her. The voices were talking about Jesus and Lazarus. She stopped near the door, but out of sight of the occupants, and listened.

"He continues to blaspheme – saying that he could build the Temple in three days!"

"He tries to make the people believe that he is The Messiah."

"We've got to get rid of him before he turns the people against us."

"We also must do away with Lazarus. I was there and saw him come out of the tomb, like he had come back from death."

"He couldn't possibly have!"

"Try to tell that to the people."

"How can we eliminate the two of them? Jesus has such a large following."

"Can we do anything while it is Passover?"

"We must think of a way. We cannot let him go on any longer."

'Do you think he could really be the Messiah as he claims?"

"Of course not!'

"But the people believe that he is."

"That is the reason he must be killed. Cut off the head and the serpent will die. If the people believe that he has come to restore our sovereignty as a nation, they could mount a rebellion against Rome and we would be held responsible for it. I, for one, do not want to be pitted against Rome, do you?"

"And look how viciously he has attacked us. Even two days ago when he raged through the Temple, upsetting the tables of the moneychangers and accusing all of us of being robbers! He called us a 'den of thieves!'"

"The question is how can we stop him – quickly – with a city bulging with his followers and all the pilgrims"

"There is someone who might help."

Rachel was horrified as she realized that these men were talking about killing Jesus and Lazarus. She knew that she must get away from here and tell someone who could do something about it. She had to get back to Benjamin's house and tell Eli. He would know what to do. Somehow she had to find the way back, but the streets were nearly empty now and those few who were still out were intent on beating the sun, which was now rapidly descending behind the hills.

As she walked down the shadowy street, she asked God to help her find her way. She was glad as she turned the corner and looked up. There she saw the Temple shining in the sun in the distance. She started toward it, knowing that she would be able to find the spice merchant's house near it.

The streets were nearly deserted now and the sun had slipped below the horizon. The streets were dark and frightening, but the Temple on top of Temple Mount still gleamed in the sun and she kept heading in that direction. She was getting tired and knew that Eli would be worried about her. She had left the house without telling anyone of her mission. How could she have been so foolish?

"Oh, Lord, how could I have been so foolish? You know me, Lord, and You know that I serve You with all my heart. Please help me to get back to my husband and family," she prayed as she walked.

She turned the next corner and looked up. Before her was the spice merchant's home. "Oh, thank You, my Lord," she breathed as she hurried toward the doors. At that moment, one of the doors opened and Rachel saw Eli come out. She ran to him and he embraced her.

When they entered the courtyard, the rest of the family gathered around them.

"What happened?"

"Where were you?"

"We were so worried about you?"

Rachel looked at the ground and felt ashamed that she had caused her husband and their hosts to worry so much about her. How could she be so thoughtless? That was the problem, she had thought only of her desire to speak with Mary and had ignored the effect her spontaneous action would have on herself and others. Now she must face them, but she also needed to tell them about the conversation she had overheard.

"I am so sorry that I caused you such anxiety," she began. "I saw someone in the street with whom I wanted to speak. I had not seen her in more than thirty years and there she was. I wasn't thinking when I ran out the door to find her. I searched for her, but she was gone by the time I got there. I tried to find her and suddenly realized that I was lost.

"I was on a deserted street," she continued, "when I heard some voices. I went toward the open door and heard some men. They were talking about killing Jesus and Lazarus."

"Lazarus!" Eli interrupted. "Why would they talk about Lazarus? Our friend Lazarus? Are you sure?"

"Yes, our friend who was raised from the dead. That is why they want to kill him, too."

"I heard," interjected Benjamin, "about the rabbi Jesus supposedly raising him, but I didn't really believe it ever happened."

"It happened," Eli assured him. Turning to Rachel, he told her to continue her story.

"I didn't listen long. I was frightened," she went on, "so I left the street and tried to find my way back here. It was so dark and there was no one in the streets who could give me directions. So I prayed for God's guidance. Then I remembered that your house was near the Temple, so I reasoned that if I kept going toward Temple Mount, I would find your house. I kept my eyes on the Mount and prayed and here I am."

"Praise be to God!" Eli cried as he again embraced Rachel. The group echoed the phrase.

"What can we do about what I heard? Who can we tell who can stop them?" she asked.

"Exactly who was speaking and what did they say?" asked Benjamin.

"I don't know who the men were. I didn't quite get to the door. When I heard the conversation, I didn't want them to know that I overheard it," she told them and then she repeated as much of the conversation as she could remember.

The group was stunned. Eli held Rachel close to him.

"I'm so glad that you are safe. You were right not to let them see you. If they are intent on murder, you were in danger," Eli said. "Who should we go to, Benjamin?"

"Not knowing who the men were, it would be dangerous to go to anyone," Benjamin began reasoning. "You might go to one of them and then we would all be in danger."

"But we must go to someone," Rachel pleaded.

"It is too late to do anything today," Eli observed, adding, "but tomorrow we will decide who to tell."

Picking up on that, Benjamin invited, "Come now, let us sup."

The Plan

Eli and Rachel arose early the next morning. They had both spent a fitful night weighing the burden of their frightening knowledge. Finally, Eli formed a plan.

"Rachel," he began, "we must send Jesse back to Bethany to warn Lazarus of the plot. He must leave immediately and he can return by the time of the seder."

"But what can we do to warn Jesus?" Rachel asked.

"We will go together to the Temple, where Jesus will likely be teaching. Then you can tell him about what you heard. The rest will be up to Him. This is all we can do," Eli answered.

"Yes," Rachel agreed, "that is the best thing to do."

Eli awoke Jesse and told him to take the donkey and ride to Bethany to warn Lazarus, then to return before sunset. The boy's excitement at being trusted with such a vital mission immediately banished his sleepiness. He quickly dressed for the journey as Eli prepared the donkey and Rachel fixed some food in a bundle for him to take to eat on the way. The boy made good time through the streets, which were sparsely populated at this early hour, and was at the city gate when it was opened for the day. From the roof of Benjamin's house, Eli and Rachel watched his progress up the Mount of Olives.

Benjamin and Miriam met them as they came down from the roof and Eli told them of the plan for the day. Miriam summoned her servant girl and soon she brought the couple some cakes and fruit to eat before they left for the Temple.

It was nearing midday when Jesus arrived at the Temple to teach. As usual, he had many people following him. Eli and Rachel joined the crowd. When he came to a spot opposite the treasuries, where people deposited their monetary gifts to the Temple, he sat down. The people crowded in as close as they could to him and sat down, too.

He sat there for a while and watched as merchants came and dropped coins, which clattered noisily down the metal tubes into the chambers. Some of them made quite a show of their contributions. Others put the coins in quietly and let the money do its own talking. Then a poor widow approached the collection place and quietly dropped two mites, the smallest coins minted, into the receptacle. They didn't make very much noise at all. The woman silently left, her head bowed. Jesus spoke:

"Truly, I say to you that this poor widow has put in more than all the rest, for all of these out of their abundance have put in offerings to God, but she out of her poverty has put in all the livelihood that she had."

The followers murmured. Jesus spoke again.

"The Lord God doesn't look at the gift you give, so much as He looks at the heart of the giver. One who wholeheartedly commits his life is much more valuable than one who merely fulfills an obligation or does the least he can. This is true for all you do in life, not just the giving of money, which is only a token of what the heart holds dear."

Rachel marveled at the truth Jesus spoke and wished that she, too, could follow Him and learn from His wisdom. After a while, the crowd began to thin out as people went off to eat their midmorning meal.

Eli and Rachel approached Jesus and asked to speak with him privately. They walked a short distance from the gathering and Rachel told him of the conversation she had overheard the previous night. Jesus didn't seem perturbed at all.

"I am grateful that you have told me about this conversation," He said. "Please do not trouble yourselves about these things. Everything will be as it is supposed to be. I am in My Father's hands and soon you will see Scripture fulfilled." He returned to those awaiting Him.

Rachel was perplexed as she and Eli turned to go. Even if she couldn't talk with Him more, she wanted to stay and listen to what He said, but Eli took her arm and led her away.

Rachel had not seen Mary in the group of followers that morning and wondered where she might be. Perhaps, she decided, she was making preparations for the Passover feast which would be observed at sundown this evening. She wondered where Jesus and Mary would celebrate.

When they reached Benjamin's house, Eli and Simon took the lambs they had brought and went to the Temple where the animals would be examined and, if unblemished, sacrificed. They joined the throng already at the Temple gates waiting for the priests to examine their lambs. When the sheep were pronounced fit for sacrifice, the men waited for the gates to be opened and the slaughter to begin. They were in the middle of the crowd and knew that they would have to wait a while for their turn.

At last the shofar, the ram's horn trumpet, sounded and the gates opened admitting about one-third of those waiting with their lambs. The shofar again sounded and the doors were closed. From the parapets and walls came the sound of Levites singing psalms to the accompaniment of reed pipes and stringed instruments.

When the shofar announced the admittance of the second group, the doors opened and the first group left. When the next crowd entered with their bleating lambs, the shofar again signaled the closing of the doors. As the men carried their lambs forward, a long row of priests awaited them. The head of each line held a gold or silver vessel. Behind him was a line of priests filling the distance between the sacrifice and the altar.

As each participant reached the priest, he slit the throat of his lamb and the priest held the vessel beneath the cut to collect the blood. When the vessel was full, it was replaced with an empty vessel to receive more blood while the filled one passed down the line behind until it reached the last priest, who splashed it on the altar, then passed the empty vessel back up the line.

With the drained lamb in hand, each man returned to the gate to await its opening after all the lambs in this group had been slaughtered. Eli and Simon were in the middle of the group. Because the process was so well orchestrated, it really didn't take long to kill the thousands of animals presented. Then the gates opened and they were on their way back to the house.

When they returned with the carcasses, the servant girl began preparing and cooking them for the evening meal. Each household would celebrate the exodus from Egyptian bondage more than 1400 years ago by completely consuming the sacrificed lamb. This celebration was remembrance of the final plague, the visit by the Angel of Death who passed over houses marked with the blood of a slain lamb, finally gaining the Jews their freedom from the oppression of Egyptian bondage.

While the men had taken the lamb to the Temple, the women had been busily preparing the remainder of the meal, so as soon as the lamb was roasted and the sun was set, the celebration would begin.

Shortly before sundown, Jesse returned and Simon's sisters, Hannah and Rebecca, and their husbands, Aaron and Elijah, with their children arrived, completing the party. When their feet were washed, they joined the others in the main room where the table had been prepared. The seder, the traditional Passover feast, would now begin. The men and boys settled themselves around the table on the lounges. The women started bringing in the dishes containing lamb, unleavened bread, bitter herbs, wine and fruit.

The story of the exodus from Egypt was told in scripture as the participants were eating the elements of the seder. As scripture describing each portion of the story was read, corresponding foods were consumed. According to those scriptures, the traditional meal began with the roasted lamb, commemorating the lambs' blood painted on the lintel and doorposts of the Israelites in Egypt eaten that night so the Angel of Death would know to pass over that house. In houses where there was no blood on the doorposts, the firstborn son died. With the lamb, unleavened bread was served. This symbolized the haste with which their ancestors had left Egypt. Bitter herbs signified the years of slavery they had endured there. The wine and fruit symbolized the abundant land to which the Lord had led them with his pillar of fire by night and cloud by day.

When the men finished their meal, the women ate – following the same ritual. It was important that no morsel of the lamb be left. Any remnants were thrown into the fire to be completely consumed. When the meal was finished, the women joined the men and they all conversed well into the night.

Deborah's family had agreed to leave Jerusalem after Passover and celebrate the Feast of Unleavened Bread, which would follow for the next seven days, at home in Bethany, so that they could tend their animals. Rachel began packing their belongings for the trip home as soon as she arose the next morning. Carefully she folded the garments they had worn and placed them in a pouch she had made to be thrown across the donkey's back.

From the street came some irate voices. She couldn't quite make out what they were saying, but their tone was disturbing. Eli, returning from preparing the donkey and arousing the young members of his family, heard them, too, and looked out the latticed window. Below he saw some Roman soldiers driving three men before them with timbers across their backs. The crowd following them was shouting angry words and calling for death. Rachel joined him at the window.

"What is happening?" she asked.

"It looks like these men are to be crucified by the Romans," Eli answered.

"Are they criminals?"

"Most likely. It seems like one of them must be worse than the other two. Look at his back. He's been scourged."

Rachel looked at the poor man. Just then he looked up to Heaven and she gasped.

"What's wrong?" Eli asked.

"That man, the one who has been scourged, looks like Jesus, the prophet who raised Lazarus. Do you think they have taken Lazarus, too?" she answered.

"I don't see him."

"Oh, that must be Jesus. There is Mary in those following. I must go to her," exclaimed Rachel as she flew out of the room, down the stairs and out the door. Eli ran after her, determined that she would not become lost again.

Once in the street, Rachel began pushing through the throng, gradually working her way up to Mary. Suddenly, Mary slumped on a doorstep, wracked with great sobs. Rachel knelt beside her and put her arms about her. Mary looked up at her face. Not a word was said. Eli stopped where the two women were and Mary saw him.

"Eli? Rachel?" she asked.

"Yes, yes," Rachel responded. "We're here. Let us help you."

"They arrested him last night and tried him. This morning they got Pilate to sentence him to death by crucifixion. That is where they are taking him," Mary sobbed. "I must go with him." She struggled to her feet and followed the still clamoring throng.

Eli took Rachel's arm and held her back from following Mary.

"Let her go. She needs to be with him. We need to go," he said firmly.

"But how can I let her go? She needs someone to lean on now," Rachel cried as she tried to pull out of his grasp.

"His followers will care for her. There is nothing you can do for her now," he replied.

"But I haven't seen her for so long and I have so much I need to know from her," Rachel pleaded, but Eli kept a tight hold on her arm as he started back through the opposing stream of humanity. Finally they reached Benjamin's house and entered the comparative quiet of the courtyard.

Benjamin and Miriam rushed to meet them and Eli told them that his family must leave soon. When he went upstairs to retrieve the pouch, Rachel sat down on the bench near the door, weeping. Miriam sat down beside her and embraced her.

"I wanted to go with her to help her," sobbed Rachel.

"Who?" inquired Miriam.

"Mary," Rachel answered. "She was my friend many years ago and I had not seen her for so very long."

"Why did you think she needed help?"

"Because they had arrested her son and were taking him to be crucified."

"Crucified?"

"I guess those men I heard night before last found a way to kill Jesus. He is her son. Jesus, the rabbi – the prophet."

"I thought that you and Eli had warned Him of the plot yesterday."

"We did, but He said that everything would be as it was supposed to be and for us not to worry about it. But I know of the anguish that awaits her," Rachel sobbed, "I lost my sons, too."

"I am so sorry, my dear," Miriam comforted her as she held Rachel in her arms.

Eli returned and Naomi, Simon, Phoebe and Jesse now stood by the door, ready to leave.

"You must go with your family and not think any more about this terrible thing," Miriam told her as she gently pulled her to her feet and gave her hand to Naomi. With subdued goodbyes, the entourage passed through the doors and headed down the street toward the city gate and the place they would meet the rest of the family for the journey home.

Redemption

The feast days were past and life had returned to normal, but Rachel was haunted by the memory of Mary struggling on her way to see her son's death. She kept wondering about this event. Was this the same child who had been born in Bethlehem? Whose birth had been announced by God's angels to the shepherds? The question would not leave her mind. If Jesus was the King of the Jews, why hadn't He changed anything? The Romans were still in control and the Jews were still in bondage to them. What was God's plan? Jesus had said that everything that would happen was according to God's will. How could God let His Son die? A cruel death at that? She tried to understand, but there were no answers to her questions.

She and Eli had been relieved when they returned home, to learn that Lazarus was unharmed, though distraught when he heard about Jesus' death. Samuel, Eli and Jesse had worked very hard this past week to ready their wares to take to the market and this morning, they were in Jerusalem. Rachel, Deborah and Sarah had spent a great deal of time together this week and Rachel knew that Eli, worried about her, had asked them to watch over her. The three women were sitting under the grape arbor Phoebe had planted so long ago shelling beans and talking about the things which needed to be done before Phoebe's betrothal celebration. They were surprised by the early return of the men from the market.

Sarah ran to meet them.

"What happened?" she asked excitedly.

"The most amazing thing," Samuel began to answer, but Eli interrupted.

"We will tell all of you as soon as we tend to the animals," he said authoritatively. Quickly the men unhitched the donkeys, put them in the pen with some hay and rolled the carts under the extended roof of the shop. The women were anxiously waiting in the arbor to hear the news.

"Go ahead, Samuel, tell them," urged Eli as they joined them in the shade of the grapevines.

"Do you remember how Jesus raised Lazarus from the dead?" he began.

"Yes, yes," chorused the women.

"Well, God raised Him as He raised Lazarus!" Samuel continued.

"He what?" asked Rachel.

"God raised Him from the dead," repeated Eli.

"Are you sure?"

"Do the authorities know about this?"

"Was he really dead?"

Eli broke into the questions. "The morning we left Jerusalem, the Romans were taking Him out on the Damascus Road to the main place for crucifying prisoners. He and the two thieves we saw with Him that morning were placed on the crosses. The thieves were tied to their crosses as they usually do it, but Jesus was nailed to his cross."

Samuel broke in, "They used big nails – one in each hand and one holding His feet together." The women cringed at the gruesome thought.

"Some of the people who were there watching told us that He said some unusual things while He was hanging there," Samuel added.

"Things like what?" asked Deborah.

"He said that His Father should forgive them for they didn't know what they were doing," answered Samuel.

"Who was He talking about?" Sarah wanted to know.

"We aren't sure, but it was probably the soldiers who were putting Him to death," said Eli. "He also told one of the thieves that he would be with Him in Paradise that day."

"How could such a man go to Paradise?" challenged Rachel.

"I don't know," Eli admitted, "unless this man was God's Son."

The group was struck into stunned silence by the statement. Each in his own mind contemplated what this could mean.

As she pieced her thoughts together, Rachel remembered the things she had been mulling over before Passover. Could this Jesus be the baby she had seen and played with in Bethlehem all those years ago? Mary had been following his entourage and when she and Eli had knelt to aid her that morning, she recognized them. She told them that the man being crucified was her son. On the night of his birth, the baby had been worshipped as the Son of God. She had heard many stories of the miraculous things He had done in the last few years – things which only God could do! Or the Son of God!

After a while, Deborah said that she was going to prepare the evening meal and Sarah, Phoebe and Rachel went to help her, for they would share the meal.

There was little conversation that evening as each person weighed the things they knew or had heard about this man who had apparently died a public death and risen again.

Rachel arose before the sun came up and walked out in the fields. They were not filled with wheat the way they had been at Bethlehem. Around Bethany, the hills were more desolate and rocky. A light tinge of green appeared on them only in the winter and spring. Many of the people had goats because they didn't require much grass and they gave milk. There was a small herd of the animals grazing on the hill just ahead of her.

A few kids scampered around the herd, but didn't seem to be interested in any particular female. She watched them play as she walked. Soon she came to a rock and sat on it. She looked up to the heavens and wondered. Is God really up there? Was Jesus His Son? Is He up there, too, now? How could she ever know and what would it mean to her if she did know for sure?

The questions kept flooding her mind. She prayed asking God for the answers to her questions. She wished that she could talk with Mary again. They had been such close friends and all these years she had missed that relationship. What unimaginable agony Mary would be going through now. Much like the agony she experienced when she lost Jacob and Reuben. If only she could see her again.

She rose from her resting place and slowly walked home. Eli was waiting for her. She hadn't gone far and he could see her from the village, so he hadn't been worried. He knew that she was trying to put the pieces together so that she could make sense of all that had happened, not only now, but in the past. Somehow they both seemed to be connected. He wondered how Rachel had known to look for Mary with Jesus, so he asked her.

"When did you know that Mary was Jesus' mother?" he asked.

Rachel looked at him with a question on her face, but answered, "I really didn't know for sure until we found her in that doorway. I had started to figure out the connection when The Prophet, Jesus, raised Lazarus. I asked Mary, Lazarus' sister, about Jesus' family and found out that his mother was named Mary and her husband was a carpenter named Joseph and that Jesus had come from Nazareth. At first,

I wasn't sure, but when I remembered that Mary and Joseph had come from Nazareth, I was more certain that Jesus was the baby who was born that wonderful night in Bethlehem."

"Everything seems to fit. But where is Joseph?" Eli asked.

"Joseph died," she replied. "What does the Scripture say about the Messiah?"

"I don't know, but I will see if the priests can help me find out. Wouldn't it be wonderful if Jesus really was The Messiah?" He paused, then added, "but if He was, why did He die without bringing us freedom?"

The Search

For the next month Eli spent as much time as he could at the synagogue looking through the Scripture for references to the Messiah. There were many and he was astonished at how many had been fulfilled by the life of Jesus. Each night he told Rachel about the passages he found that day. Little by little, both of them became more convinced that they had witnessed the birth night of the Messiah and had been privileged to be with Him intimately when He was a baby.

As new questions about Jesus came to her mind, Rachel would ask Mary or Martha about them. It was good to have someone to talk with who knew Jesus as a friend and had heard Him speak about many things. As Rachel's belief in her supposition grew, Mary and Martha also seemed to grow into a deeper understanding of Jesus and His mission.

One day, two of Jesus' disciples came for a visit with Mary, Martha and Lazarus. John and James had been to their home several times with Jesus and knew that He loved them, so they came to give them good news. Not only had Jesus risen from the dead, but He was alive and had appeared in their midst many times.

Although they had witnessed Jesus ascending to Heaven, He had told them that on an appointed day, the Day of Pentecost, all the believers were to meet in a certain place in Jerusalem. The three of them were invited to attend the gathering of followers and they immediately made plans to go.

When Mary, Martha and Lazarus returned to Bethany after their trip to Jerusalem on the Day of Pentecost, they had changed. Rachel didn't exactly know how they were different, but they were. She drew Mary aside and asked her to relate what had happened when they went to Jerusalem. Mary gladly shared the wondrous story with her friend.

"Soon after sunrise on the appointed day," Mary began, "Martha, Lazarus and I arrived at the location. There were a great many people there already. The place was filled with lively conversation as those present discussed their expectations for this event. There were many theories on exactly what would happen, but no one, including the disciples, knew what it would be.

"Someone started to sing a song of praise and soon the whole body of people lifted their voices to praise God together. There was a serene yet supernatural power in the room and everyone seemed to be under its control. Suddenly there was a mighty rush of wind blowing through the place. Everyone became silent.

"Someone pointed to John's head and shouted, 'Look, he's on fire!' All eyes turned to John. There was a flame rising out of his head. Looking around, we saw that everyone had a flame coming out of their head. In a panic, we poured out into the street and found ourselves talking in foreign tongues to people passing by. The passersby, who were of many different nationalities, understood what we were saying because we were speaking in their native tongues – languages we did not know.

"The Holy Spirit which Jesus had promised to send had come upon the crowd of believers. We were proclaiming the glory of God and the Messiah to people from all over the world. Many of those who heard, believed and took back the good news when they returned to their homes."

"Can you still speak in the language you spoke there?" asked the eager Rachel.

"I don't know," Mary answered, "I don't even know what I said, and when the person I was talking to answered, I heard it in my language. It was amazing! Everyone could understand everyone else! John told us that the Holy Spirit had come on us as Jesus promised and that we would be able to converse with anyone about Jesus and to proclaim Him as Messiah and they would understand what we were saying even though we didn't know their language!" Rachel was awed by this revelation.

She thanked Mary and ran back home to tell Eli and the children what Mary had said of her extraordinary experience. "Could this be how Jesus is to be King? By teaching the whole world to live peaceably together? Perhaps when the Romans realize that Jesus came to bring peace, we won't have to drive them out. We will be able to live in peace with them," she concluded.

"I'm not so sure that the Romans will believe that," answered Jesse.

"But perhaps they might," his father added.

"Now, I am certain that Jesus truly is the Messiah," Rachel said.

"Don't you mean 'was'?" questioned Eli.

"No," Rachel answered, "Is! He is risen and is the living Son of God – the Savior of us all. I praise the Lord God Almighty!"

Rachel walked out into the fields. She looked toward the hills and a bit of Scripture came to her mind. "I will look unto the hills from whence comes my help. My help comes from the Lord."

For so long she had wondered about many things concerning the baby born so long ago in the stable-cave, who the shepherds had claimed was the Son of God. She marveled at the calm she had felt around Mary and her baby. She reasoned that God must have warned her neighbors about Herod's terrible slaughter and by their untimely and unexpected departure, saved His Son's life so that He could fulfill His mission as foretold in the Scriptures. She wondered if Mary had regretted not warning Rachel and Eli about possible danger, but dismissed this thought when she realized that she probably didn't know what had happened in the aftermath of their sojourn in Bethlehem. Suddenly she understood that Mary and Joseph were probably following God's directive and if they hadn't Herod might have thwarted God's plan for His Son.

Rachel had begun to piece things together as she talked with Mary and Martha about their brother's miraculous return from the dead. At that time she began to feel strange stirrings in her soul. She almost felt as if she had known the Rabbi, even though they had never met. Then there were the Scriptures Eli found regarding the Messiah, which this Jesus had fulfilled.

When she saw Mary in Jesus' group of followers, she impulsively chased after them and found herself lost. The clandestine conversation she overheard on that dark and silent street had first caught her attention because of her friend's brother's name, but it was linked to Jesus by His action. Then when she finally had a minute meeting with Mary, who she was sure she had known in Bethlehem, and Mary recognized her and Eli, Rachel knew that the Rabbi – the Prophet – was the same child born that night now grown into a man.

And lastly, having heard the wonderful account of Mary, Martha and Lazarus' experience in Jerusalem and seeing the radiance that was around them, she was certain! Truly that baby was the Son of God! Rachel fell to her knees.

"I praise You, oh my Lord," she prayed looking heavenward. "You have sent Your Son to visit us here and to show both Your love for us and Your plan for our lives. We don't understand Your ways – why You would let Him suffer so much and die so cruelly, but we trust You to know what is best. All of my life, I have trusted in You, even through the dark times. I do not know why You allowed me to touch Your Son's life in His infancy, but I thank You for the honor. I was so angry with You when I lost my sons, but I know how Mary must feel right now. Help her through this time as You helped me through my darkness.

"If only I could have known Your Son better. I would have liked to hear His message to us and learned at His feet, but that was not to be. Thank You for drawing me to Him again. Through Him, I have been twice touched by You. Thank You for the Scriptures which prophesied His coming – and His death. Thank you for Jesus. Oh Lord, I am so sorry that I could not do more to spare Him from that terrible death."

She was sobbing when God answered through the voice of Eli, who had come to her when he had seen her kneel and had overheard her prayer

"Everything went according to God's plan. According to the Scriptures, Jesus was to 'be led as a lamb to the slaughter' but in so doing He willingly allowed Himself to suffer that death to atone for your sins and mine. That was why he came in the first place.

"One of King David's psalms says, 'You have turned for me my mourning into dancing; You have put off my sackcloth and clothed me with gladness.' Come now, let us celebrate His life. Truly, we have been twice touched – twice blessed."

Rachel rose from her knees and the couple embraced each other, both sobbing as the full realization of the greatness of God's love enveloped them. A sense of great peace settled over them as they made their way home.

At last, Rachel's questions had all been answered in the person of Jesus of Nazareth and she knew that her life would never be the same again.

Jesus was The Answer!

Jesus is *still* The Answer!

Only

She was only a teenaged mother-to-be,
    Just one of the weary crowd.
        He was only a simple carpenter
           As he lead her down the road.
               They were only following orders
                   Issued by a king in Rome,
                       And they only found a stable
                           As their temporary home.
They were only sleepy shepherds
    Tending their flocks that night,
        When from the realms of glory
           They beheld a glorious sight.
               Bands of angels announced it,
                   Heaven's radiance unfurled.
                       It was the only announcement
                           Of the birth that changed the world.
It was only a star in the sky
    That brought the kings from afar.
        They followed it night after night
           'Til it brought them to the door.
               He was only a tiny baby,
                   But the kings before Him bowed
                       And gave Him their costly gifts –
                       Frankincense, myrrh and gold.
It was only one time in history –
    Now the world isn't the same,
        For only the birth of this baby
           Could light the eternal flame.
               He grew. He taught. He died. He rose.
                   Best of all, He still lives today.
                       He wants all to join Him, for to find
                         Life eternal, He is the only way.

www.ingramcontent.com/pod-product-compliance
Lightning Source LLC
Chambersburg PA
CBHW020149180626
46810CB00004B/1802